Dearsie

Rebecca Norton Miller

Aurora Books, an imprint of Eco-Justice Press, L.L.C.

Aurora Books
P.O. Box 5409 Eugene, OR 97405
www.ecojusticepress.com

Dearsie
Written by Rebecca Norton Miller

Cover design by Wendy L. Stasolla

Library of Congress Control Number: 2018964447
ISBN 978-1-945432-28-6

This story is dedicated with love and respect to Beverly Broy Leidel, the sole surviving member of the family the story is about. You are living history, and a loving presence.

Chapter One – Belgium

There was a time when I didn't exist. There was a time when only Annie and Jim Bill giggled in the hallways and cried in the night; a time when I hadn't yet made my appearance.

There was a time before me, but I don't remember it. I have only stories and photographs, Annie looking solemn and stern, maybe even disbelieving and scornful, Jim Bill with his ever-present smile and twinkling eyes.

That is how I believe they existed before I became their baby sister. Because I've seen that downcast, furrowed brow, that doubting-Thomas, steely gaze. And I've seen that devil-may-care, here-comes-trouble grin. Apparently those tell-tale expressions predated me, vexed and delighted Mummy and Daddy before they ever laid eyes on me.

I was born on January 20, 1930. I don't remember being born, or even being a baby. But I remember being happy and small and carefree.

And I remember all of us together. Those were some gay times back on Lowther Road in southwest London. That is where we lived, Annie, Jim Bill, and I, with Hoop and Huck. And though Hoop and Huck may sound like two characters from a cartoon to you, that was what we sometimes called Mummy and Daddy.

We always had nicknames in our family. "Hoop" and "Huck" for our parents. Jimmy was "Jim Bill," short for James William.

My given name is Beverly, quite a sophisticated name. But I always liked it when Huck would call me "Dearsie," a nickname just for me.

They say I was a good baby, a happy baby. I didn't cry much, and I smiled and laughed and let my older brother and sister entertain me, hold me, and offer their fingers up for grabbing. Mummy said I was the last one because she knew she couldn't do any better, that she had all the children she was meant to have. I knew she loved me, even if her attention wandered after the initial thrill of my infancy wore off.

I have always tried to remain positive and sweet. I know that's what Mummy would want.

I recall those early days on Lowther Road only as vignettes.

In the summers, Huck loved working on his many, many rose bushes (I think there were about 57), tending them and using the hose to sprinkle the soil. Their blooms were coral and magenta and butter-yellow.

When the summer temperature reached what we considered a horrendous 70° F in London's climate, Hoop would let us put on our bathing suits. We three kids would play outside till after dark, enjoying the freedom of summer and an occasional spray from the hose from Huck, causing us to squeal and cry, "Do it again!"

At bedtime, Hoop would lean out of the upstairs window and call to us. Then Huck would turn the hose on her, eliciting raucous laughter from Daddy and Hoop's protests of, "Stop it!" as she grabbed her hair, so carefully secured with bobby pins, and backed out of view.

Sometimes we'd head south to Southampton or Brighton Beach to frolic in the surf and sand. Our favorite, though, was Ostende Beach. At the fancy hotel there, we'd have shrimp croquettes—flaky pastries with tiny shrimp inside. Sis and Jimmy were my closest friends, and we three did everything together. Hoop and Huck encouraged our friendship, and took pride in how well we three got on.

Weekend outings included big Hyde Park, where we picnicked and climbed tall, handsome old trees. In those "olden" days, a picnic was simply boiled eggs, sardines, tomatoes, and bread.

Sunday mornings were great fun. We'd scramble out of our dormitory (all three of us in one room with beds lined up) and race to Huck's room, where we would pile onto his big bed. Jimmy had a boxing bag strung up in the frame of Daddy's bedroom door so he could proceed with his sparring. Jimmy had lots of energy and Daddy said it was good for him to exercise it out, along with any anger, frustration, or just feelings of wanting to kick something, which Jimmy sometimes did.

The colder weather leant itself to outdoor adventures in the snow. Indoor distractions involved staying warm and entertained. We'd huddle with Hoop like a mama duck and her ducklings, the four of us gathering around the little stove in the hallway of our house as

Hoop read Aesop's fables to us until the doorbell rang in the early, dark London evenings.

The doorbell signaled that Daddy was home. We would scamper out to the vestibule, converge upon our father, and hide beneath his long, thick overcoat.

He would then challenge Hoop, asking, "And where are the children?"

We would dissolve into giggles, as though she couldn't see the six extra legs protruding below the hem of his coat.

Hoop and Huck were willing participants in our game. It felt safe under Huck's coat, holding onto his legs. And it was a fine, adventurous feeling as well, being in the dark, unable to see, only guessing at the faces Hoop might pull as she pretended not to know where we'd gone.

There was a playful lilt to both their voices as they played out their roles, Huck indignant and somewhat accusatory and Hoop, feigning surprise, embarrassment, and ignorance as to our whereabouts.

"Why Mr. Broy, they were only just here! Where *could* they have got to?"

"Mrs. Broy, how can you possibly have *lost* three children! It isn't as if they're mice, for heaven's sake! We must find them at once!"

And on it would go, until finally we'd get to laughing so hard or feel the need to burst out and show ourselves. We'd duck out from under the hem of the coat, calling out, "We're here! We're here!" And our parents would look relieved and happy to see us.

At Christmas time, Hoop would decorate our house with holly and candles, and we would trim the tree with popcorn and cranberries, sewn on a thread. Mummy would let us use her thimbles as we pushed the sharp needles through the firm berries and toughened kernels.

Our gifts were clothes—sturdy socks, new dresses—or books, dolls, and rolling hoops. One year we got Plasticine, which we used to model all kinds of creatures and outlandish creations.

Jimmy got a Meccano set one year, and spent hours building vehicles and structures and then destroying them just so he could rebuild them.

Hoop had us pose for a picture as a gift to Huck one Christmas. We three wanted to smile and wave, but the photographer was rather stern and required stillness and serious faces. He kept mumbling to me, "Sit up, then, dear," in a voice that lacked any sort of warmth.

In the end, we rather thought Daddy would enjoy the picture because this errant display of a character we simply did not possess would surely make him laugh out loud.

Earlier that year, I had taken a bit of a tumble. Mummy and Daddy were entertaining, and we kids were playing a rousing game of hide and seek when I backed up to a second story window and fell right out, resulting in a fractured skull and a concussion. I don't remember much, only that I had to hold very still and Mummy held my hand as dearly as she ever had.

But all that happened in London. When I was six, we moved to Brussels, Belgium, where Daddy had a new post as the American Consul. Mummy had selected our large apartment, having gone ahead of us to find it. She'd said it was only fair to Daddy that in Brussels, he be closer to his office; in London, he commuted an hour and a half back and forth. Also, she'd wanted a place big enough to accommodate the entertaining she and Daddy would sometimes need to do.

Our new address was Apartment 68, Quartier Rubens, Residence Palace, Rue de la Loi, near the Parc Cinquantenaire. We were way up on the top with the entire eighth floor to ourselves. While in America, the first floor is considered as "1," in Belgium, you do not count the ground floor, or *rez de chausse*. After the ground floor, eight floors later, you're on the "eighth floor."

We each had our own bedroom in Brussels, and each bedroom had a wash basin for grimy faces and sweaty brows. Mine was chipped in one spot due to a brush with my elbow one time while chasing Jim Bill out of my room in a game. Its loud clatter to the floor paused our game only momentarily, but the chip became a constant reminder to Mummy of our reckless nature.

Mummy's room was at the near end of a short hall with us, and Daddy had his own suite at the other end. At night, Jimmy would walk me along the dark hall to my bedroom, telling me which kind of horrible spook would be waiting. It was during these times that I most wished Jimmy might be a little more sensitive. He knew I believed in ghosts, even though I pretended not to.

The building itself was luxurious, with a doorman and a fountain in the courtyard, and a garage for all the fancy cars. It was made up of four "quarters," buildings essentially, that all huddled together high above the city, easily seen from a distance.

Mummy went ahead of us to set up the apartment, and by the time we arrived she was in the midst of hanging pictures and setting vases on surfaces. There were pictures of our family, but there were also many pictures of Mummy, who was quite photogenic. I'd often stare at them, studying every shadow.

I hoped I'd look like her when I grew up. In certain photographs, she looked like a princess. There was one of her being presented at St. James Court to King George V and Queen Mary. In it, she wore above-the-elbow white silk gloves and a long white gown and veil, more resembling a wedding gown than what she wore the day she married Daddy. The photo was an ever-present reminder of not just her beauty, but her connections.

She had an elegant way of holding herself, an aloofness in her eyes, and a demure smile. She also had impeccable manners, and knew just how to speak to a king and queen, and how to curtsy.

Mummy had been invited to court in 1930, just after I'd been born. It was traditional to present ambassadors, consulates, and other foreign dignitaries and their wives to the ruler of a country. In this case, the rulers were Their Majesties in London. However, she'd put it off an entire year because she didn't want to be presented to Their Majesties after just having had a baby.

I went to my first school when we moved to Belgium, an American school called Washington Hall. I was excited to be going to school like Annie and Jim. Up until that time, I had been learning at home with Mummy, as had Annie and Jim before me. I anticipated making new friends and learning about the world. I felt like an explorer with new horizons in my sights.

It's in Belgium that my story truly begins. And with some of the hijinx we three Musketeers got into, well, I suppose it's no wonder Mummy left and never came back.

Chapter Two - Hijinx

I was dreaming. A happy, lilting voice from just over a hill was calling to me, "Dearsie! Dearsie!" I was running toward it, laughing and skipping, wearing my favorite dress. I felt as light as air and I never ran out of breath or grew tired as I ran. It felt exhilarating. I knew that if I could just reach the hill, climb it, and look down, I'd be able to see who was calling and why. As I began to crest the hill, I woke with a not altogether unpleasant start.

The morning light was coming through the windows, throwing pale stripes onto my bed covers and across my eyes. I felt full of energy, and maybe just a little mischief. I knew it was going to be an adventurous kind of day. I felt more alert than usual, as though there were springs in my feet. There was a tingle just under my skin and my heart was fluttering like a bird.

I never knew, on any given day, what Jimmy or Annie might have planned. Maybe today we'd play "Stalking Sue," a favorite game Annie had come up with. Jimmy and I would ride our bicycles throughout the apartment, looking out for a white handkerchief on the floor, the sign that something was about to happen. We would pedal at breakneck speed, racing down long stretches, squealing around corners and past the many rooms. The fact that we nearly crashed several times made it all the more exciting. And once we'd see the handkerchief on the floor, the suspense would be nearly unbearable.

Annie usually did one of three things: jump out in front of us, causing us to veer wildly and nearly knock over furniture or hit framed pictures; turn the radio on suddenly and quite loudly, which made us jump right off our bicycle seats; or, just for dramatic effect, walk by slowly in a nearby room, with solemn expression and a veil over her face, pretending to be a spook. Jimmy would ride straight towards her to run her down, but her ghost impression was convincing enough that I would ride as far away as I could.

Of course, the last time we'd played, Diany had been at the end of the hallway, hands on hips. She had quickly put a stop to that game. Spoilsport.

Jean Diany Servais was our governess. She was quite lovely, really, and spoiled us rotten. When we first came to Belgium, we had Molly. But Molly didn't last. No one *ever* lasted. Jimmy would always act naughty and kick them in the shins, and they would leave in a huff.

But Diany was different. She was kind and beautiful, with dark, silky hair and an open smile. We quite liked her. She played Monopoly with us when Daddy threw an official party, helping us to stay out of the way while Daddy and Mummy were entertaining dignitaries.

As the American Consul in Brussels, Daddy held a very important post, and he had very important friends. When they'd come to dinner, we children would eat dinner in the study, and sometimes we'd get a special treat. I shall never forget the delicious frozen coffee ice cream we once got, and the way it sat on my tongue, all smooth and creamy and cold. I let each spoonful rest there while it slowly melted into a cool, silky blanket.

One time, Sis and I peeked out through the doorway to spy on the party. I think the men had been drinking quite a lot because they had gotten quite silly. They were playing music, and dancing with one another. We saw the Vice Consul giggling like a schoolgirl as he danced a jitterbug in the foyer.

Sis and I looked at one another and began to giggle so much that Diany had to quickly shut the door so they wouldn't hear us. Then Jimmy started twirling us around and we clinked our water glasses together and laughed in our best imitation of giddy, drunken dignitaries. Diany tried to look stern, but she was laughing behind her hand. I saw it.

Mr. Cudahy, the Ambassador to Belgium and Luxembourg, once invited us to attend a party in his home. There, we kids had our first taste of champagne. It tickled my nose before I ever tasted it, and then my nose wrinkled up when I did. I didn't like the champagne much. But it was so exciting being included, I drank my small glass down with everyone else. I was rewarded with a dizzy, giggly feeling that turned into drowsiness soon after.

On this adventurous day, however, I hopped out of bed and went to see if Jimmy was up. He and I had always been partners in crime.

Whatever Jimmy thought of, I would do, because his ideas were quite exciting. He was generally full of surprises, and I loved surprises.

As I opened my bedroom door I could hear urgent, insistent voices from the other end of the hall. Daddy's low basso voice, and Mummy's persistent, even one. I could always tell who was winning an argument. If Mummy's voice got quiet and stopped, I knew she was either giving up or saving her energy for a later battle. If Daddy's voice got louder and doors started to slam, I knew Daddy was giving up or was going to regroup.

It sounded like Mummy was winning this time. She was staying even and calm, and Daddy was getting louder. I heard a couple of words, like "opportunity" and "mistreatment" from Mummy, and "foolish" and "you're their mother!" from Daddy.

Just then, an arm reached out and grabbed me, pulling me into a doorway. It was Jimmy, and he was all smiles and trouble.

"Come with me, Little Girl!" He had a maniacal look in his eye and something hidden in one hand that he kept behind his back. His scruffy hair covered one eye and his shirt was buttoned all wrong. I immediately followed him into his room. I trusted Jimmy with my life, and I knew he would always have something planned that would either get us into trouble or nearly so.

"What have you got, Jim Bill?" I whispered, none too quietly.

"Just you wait and see!" he said, dragging me towards the opposite end of the room near the window. He cracked the window open just a bit, which required the use of both hands. As he pushed on the sash, I caught the briefest glimpse of the small box in his hand.

"First, you must swear to secrecy!" he said, turning to me and looking quite solemn for one who took very little seriously. His eyes were hooded, and his brow was stern. "Do you, Beverly Hite Broy, solemnly swear, beyond torture and death, to keep this secret? Even from Annie?"

Normally, I'd have agreed immediately. But this last bit about keeping it from Annie meant it was *very* serious indeed. But, as I've mentioned, I trusted Jimmy to the ends of the earth. So I nodded.

"Say it!" he whispered, with only the hint of a smile at one corner of his pursed lips and his eyes all wild and large.

"I swear!" I whispered, truly being quiet this time.

Jimmy tucked the box into his shirt, scrambled down on hands and knees, and began crawling towards his bed. He looked quite silly, shuffling along like an oversized baby, and I began to giggle behind my hand.

Jimmy turned his head, his eyes even wilder than before, and said, "This is no laughing matter, Beverly! Lives were put in danger to obtain this secret! Now, on all fours, and step to!"

I got down on my hands and knees and started to scramble after Jimmy. My nightgown kept getting caught under my knees as I crawled towards him, and several times I had to pause to tug it out from beneath.

By the time I reached him, Jimmy had already gotten halfway under his bed, turning over onto his back and using his feet to scootch himself further and further under. I followed suit, turning over onto my backside first, then laying down, careful not to bang my head on the bed frame. I imagined us hiding from enemy spies as we scrambled beneath brush in the woods. But there were only dust bunnies, a couple pieces of crumpled paper, and one lonely shoe sharing our space.

I got myself next to Jimmy, with only our feet sticking out from beneath the bed. He turned his head to me and stared into my eyes. I saw little, as it was dim beneath the bed, and his room wasn't that bright to begin with. But I could feel the intensity of his gaze. I heard him shuffle his hands as he moved within the limited space and brought the box he'd been hiding out from under his shirt and up between our two faces.

"These are St. Michel cigarettes, and—"

I gasped before he could finish his sentence. I may have been the youngest Broy in the house, but I knew we were not allowed to smoke.

Jimmy shushed me and continued, "Beverly, you and I are going to cross the line and smoke! Are you in?"

I knew I shouldn't, and I wasn't even sure I wanted to. But the mere fact that it wasn't allowed, and that somehow Jimmy had got hold of them and had included *me* in his crime and trusted *me* to keep it secret was all quite intoxicating. So, after a heartbeat's pause, I nodded vigorously.

"I can't hear you, Broy!" Jimmy taunted.

"Yes! Yes, I'll do it! I'll do it! But, Jim Bill, do you have matches too?" I asked sheepishly, thinking this was indeed something we would have to keep secret.

Jimmy hesitated for a moment, then admitted, "Well...no. But if we put them in our mouths and wet them with our tongues, we can taste the tobacco. Then, if we use our imaginations and suck really hard, we can fill our breathing with the taste, if not the actual smoke."

I was not at all disappointed or deterred by this news. I had actually been a little worried about lighting matches, especially in such close quarters and with crumpled papers nearby. I waited til Jimmy pulled out a cigarette and placed it in my hand. Then he pulled out another for himself.

"Let's be Consuls!" I said, hoping Jimmy wouldn't mind me adding to the details of our charade.

"Right then!" he said, and put the cigarette at a jaunty angle in his mouth. I could see the white outline of it hanging from his lips and hear his altered pronunciation as he spoke around the cigarette, trying to hold it between his teeth and lips without it falling.

"What word do you hear about the transfer?" he asked, his words clipped and restrained from the effort of holding the cigarette.

I wasn't entirely sure what a transfer was, but it sounded like something one did on a train, so I replied, "It was good, very good. Everyone arrived on time!"

Jimmy snickered, then said, "Quite right!" He took a long drag of his cigarette, then slowly removed it and made a long hissing sound as he blew imaginary smoke out of his mouth.

"Nice smoke rings," I added, for colorful detail. Then I sucked on my own cigarette. A couple bits of tobacco got onto my tongue, but I didn't think spitting them out would be in character, so I courageously kept them in my mouth, tasting the sweetness of them and wondering if eating them would make me sick.

I was thinking about the time Jimmy and I had taken off without permission on Jimmy's scooter back in Barnes when we ran away to the Thames. Mummy sent a bobby after us who'd lectured us on safety and obeying rules, but he did it with kindness. Mummy hadn't been nearly as forgiving as the policeman.

But getting caught never stopped us having adventures or thinking up ideas for them. I turned my head to Jimmy, who seemed lost in thought, maybe thinking up our next adventure even then, and I felt a surge of camaraderie and affection. I removed my cigarette and blew a long, loving stream of pretend smoke towards him.

As I let my mind wander, moving the tobacco bits around my mouth with my tongue, I heard the door to Jimmy's room open. Realizing that our feet were still quite visible, I yanked mine in bumping my knee on the bed frame, and yelping in pain. Jimmy didn't bother pulling in his feet. He knew we were caught.

I heard footsteps and could see the hem of a slightly worn nightgown and two squarish feet. It was Sis.

"Well, what mischief have you two gotten into now?" She sounded slightly more irritated than the situation really warranted, especially since she didn't even know yet what we were up to.

"Come on out, then," she said, dragging me by my feet from under the bed. My nightgown started to ride up my back. I yanked at the hem to keep my undergarments from being exposed. In humiliation, I squealed and dropped my cigarette. Jimmy scooted himself out, cigarette still hanging lazily from his lips.

"How's tricks?" he asked her, sitting up, taking the cigarette from his mouth, and pretending to tap off the ashes.

Annie did not look pleased. "Were you two *smoking*?" she asked.

I looked down at my feet on the carpet, still adjusting my nightgown around my hips. I thought I'd let Jimmy do the talking.

"Come, come, Sis. It's just for fun. We've had a little taste of them, but no harm done."

"I am going to tell Daddy about this!" She made no move to leave, however.

"Why are you so angry?" Jimmy asked. "No one died!"

"There are more important things going on in this world than your silly games!" she shouted. I looked up and noticed her face becoming redder. It occurred to me that perhaps she was angry we had gone on an adventure without her.

"We were playing spy. We have more if you want to try one," I offered, looking up from under my lashes.

"Decisions are being made, and you two want to pretend you're carefree adults, smoking and playing children's games."

I crinkled my brow. This last bit perplexed me as we were, after all, children.

"What decisions?" Jimmy asked in a suspicious tone. But Annie didn't continue. Jimmy had stood up by now, and tried to give Annie a gentle shove, his usual playful way of knocking her off her high horse and reminding her she was one of us. But Annie wasn't having it.

"That's it. I'm telling, and you two are in for it!"

And with that, she left, not even shutting the door behind her.

"Jimmy, should we hide the cigarettes?" I asked, a little more frantically than I'd intended.

"Maybe," he answered distractedly. "But what do you suppose has gotten Sis's bonnet so full of bees?"

"Maybe she's jealous because we didn't ask her to try the cigarettes with us?"

"Maybe..." Jimmy's mind seemed to be in the process of figuring something out, but then, just as quickly, he flashed his smile and said, "Well, Broy, no turning back now. We'll have to face the music, and remember, we mustn't reveal any state secrets!"

I nodded and saluted Jimmy, thinking that might be the appropriate thing to do in such a situation.

Jimmy slid his slightly damp cigarette back in the small orange box and held out his hand for mine. It had fallen on the floor during my most ungraceful removal from beneath the bed. I crouched down and retrieved it, handing it over to Jimmy, and he slid mine in as well. Then, he put the box under his mattress and winked at me.

"You never know," he said, a sly twinkle in his eye. "We may need these if we're imprisoned for a while!"

Chapter Three – Repercussions

Annie was true to her word and told Hoop and Huck about our digression, but Daddy seemed distracted and only muttered that we oughtn't to be smoking or wasting money on cigarettes. I chose to believe that since we really hadn't smoked them, the crime wasn't all that serious.

Mummy, on the other hand, was quite serious and focused. She made us all sit down, even Annie.

"I haven't any tolerance for such behavior," she started. "Well-bred children don't go around smoking cigarettes or lying beneath beds in the dust and dirt. I absolutely forbid you from any such activity in the future. Have I made myself clear?"

We all muttered "yes" and "of course" and "so sorry, Mummy." But I'm pretty sure Jimmy had his fingers crossed, and Annie seemed indignant to be included in the first place. She had her arms crossed and she was looking directly at *me*, as though I were the one who'd started it! Her lips were pursed and her glare was like ice.

I found myself watching as if in a dream. I took in Mummy's hair, her skin, her eyes, her lips. I observed her hands in her lap, and her smoothed skirt. She looked perfect, even as she was chastising us.

Mummy was considered to be quite a beautiful woman; I heard people say it all the time. She had fine clothes and an impressive collection of hats, and her hair was always perfectly in place. Her skin was smooth and even, and her eyes were dark and deep-set. Her lips looked like someone had drawn them on, so perfect were their lines.

Right now, they were set firm and hard. But I noted that, even when angry, and even when at home with only the family to see her, she was put together as though at any moment, guests would be arriving.

Right now, though, she had a steely glare in her eyes. I saw the disappointment on her face, not just that we'd misbehaved, but that we'd perhaps interrupted her day. Her tone of voice implied we'd failed miserably to be perfect children. At times like this, it wasn't beauty that I saw: it was power. It was a certain intractability that could not be dissuaded, and that didn't tolerate anything remotely threatening to tarnish her image.

We started to get up because we thought Hoop was done, but she raised her hand and said, "Please stay. I need to talk to you about some things."

We all shared a look with one another that said, "What are we in trouble for *now*?"

"You may have noticed that my neuralgia has only been getting worse since we've been here." Mummy stopped and rubbed her jaw, wincing in pain just for emphasis.

I had learned what the word "neuralgia" meant after hearing it the first time, and how to spell it. It had to do with the nerves in the teeth and jaws.

"My headaches have only intensified, and my teeth are in sorry shape. I've been to the dentist, but he does not seem to understand the complexities of my mouth, nor the seriousness of my situation."

At this statement, she looked at us almost conspiratorially, as if to gauge our reaction. But I'm not sure any of us knew quite where this was going, so we just stared.

"There are some highly skilled dentists back in America," she added.

Annie sat up a little straighter at this, eyes lifting from her lap to Mummy's face. I think she understood something, at least sooner, if not more, than either Jimmy or I did.

"I will be traveling back to America as soon as my papers are in order and your father and I can make arrangements. There, I will get my teeth fixed, and then be back before you can even realize I am gone."

I looked at Annie, then at Jimmy, wanting to follow their lead on this new information. I wasn't quite sure I was understanding all the implications. Annie looked down at her hands, which were fidgeting in her lap, and Jimmy took a big breath.

"How long will it take?" Jimmy finally asked.

"Well, of course, there is no telling exactly," Mummy replied. "I will have to find the right dentist, then I'll have to get the appointments, and then I'll have to have some procedures, I'm sure, after which there may be some recovery time involved, which means, of course, that

I wouldn't be able to travel straightaway. It might even be multiple procedures, so I couldn't say exactly. But dear Jimmy, you needn't worry. Your father will be here with you, and dear Diany will see to your every need in my absence."

At this, I sort of hiccupped. It wasn't that I was worried I'd miss her; Mummy had always been a very busy woman with lots of teas and socials and suppers and women's club meetings. She was gone from home a lot, and when she was home, she and Daddy were often entertaining (when they weren't arguing).

Diany was the one who made sure we got fed, did our homework, and got us to bed. Diany took us shopping when we needed new shoes or when errands needed to be run. But something about Mummy's uncertainty had me a little off-kilter.

One thing about Mummy was she *always* knew what was what. If you were to ask her who should be the next U.S. congressman or senator, she would confidently supply a name (complete with biography and political leanings); if you were to ask her about public policy she would have an opinion, and there was no arguing with it. If you were to ask what to serve the guests for dinner, she would tell Hilaria, our cook, exactly what to make, how much, and to what temperature it should be warmed.

So Mummy not giving a definite answer made everything feel unbalanced, like when you walk on a pond not knowing if the ice has frozen thick enough to skate on it. Something was off.

But before we could ask any more questions, she stood up, straightened her skirt, patted a hair back in place, and said, "Well, then! Off with you, children! Give your mother a kiss and then on with your day!"

She stooped a little with one cheek turned and accepted a kiss from each of us as we were dismissed. I could smell the faint perfume of her eau de toilette as I took my turn, dutifully pressing my lips to her smooth cheek. Then she walked out of the room, humming a wandering tune.

Chapter Four – Respite

Over the next few weeks, life went on as usual. We went to school, did our studies, played Monopoly, and got into the appropriate amount of mischief. Mummy did not leave right away. I suppose it was because it takes time to plan a trip. She continued entertaining, having teas, going to meetings, and arguing with Daddy. We even all went on the occasional day trip. I think we had mostly forgotten about her departure.

One fine spring day we three found ourselves in search of something to do. Daddy was at work, Mummy was out to tea, and our school work was done. We were looking at one another, no one particularly inspired, when Sis said, "Let's surprise Diany!"

Sis was back to playing games with us after the hubbub from the cigarette incident had died down. She'd even started coming up with a few of her own schemes and ideas.

She stood up and started walking towards her room. Something about the confident lift of her chin made Jimmy and I follow without question.

Annie walked right up to her window and pushed it open wide. Just outside was a stone ledge that was rounded like a gutter, but shallow and wide enough to walk on.

"Let's go out on the ledge, just round the corner a bit," Annie said. "I think Diany is in the next room writing letters." Because it was Annie's idea, I think Jimmy and I both surmised it couldn't be too foolhardy.

We climbed through the window, Sis first, then me, then Jim Bill. We walked slowly along the ledge. I wasn't scared—well, not a lot. Jim Bill said not to look down, and since we were on the top floor, I felt sure he must be wisely advising me. We walked just around the corner, one hand touching the building, the other extended for balance.

Diany, however, was not sitting at the desk as we'd imagined. We remained in place, waiting. Perhaps she had gone to get a drink, or perhaps her pen had run out of ink.

We took the opportunity to slowly turn our heads and see what we could see from this view. While we couldn't quite see the Parc Cinquantenaire, with its lovely arches, curved museums, and green lawn, we could see the other buildings around us, and in the distance, the railroad tracks with the occasional train going by. Inside the study, we could see Diany's desk, her journal and pen, some letter-writing papers, and a cup of tea gone cold. However, Diany was nowhere to be seen.

After we'd spent a few moments getting used to the idea of being so far off the ground on such a narrow space, our hearts stopped thumping. With no sightings of Diany, we even began to feel bored. We slowly turned, reversed our steps back around the corner, and went in through the bedroom window in reverse order, Jim Bill, then me, then Sis.

We tried again a couple days later, this time better prepared. We had decided it didn't matter so much whether or not Diany saw us; it just seemed like a decent adventure. This time, we were armed with paper and pens, and feeling more confident.

Jimmy made paper darts and flew them off the ledge. Annie and I wrote notes, some including our phone number, and tossed them over the side. They said things like, "I am an orphaned bird! Please help!" and, "This message is from the sky. Look up and see your fortune in the clouds." We pretended we were stranded on a desert island and the notes were our pleas for help and rescue.

We played "I Spy," having to improvise when the item we chose was too small to identify from a distance. We ate squares of chocolate Sis had stowed in her pocket. We closed our eyes to think of adjectives to best describe the experience (Sis thought "heavenly"; Jim Bill rather held onto "velvety smooth," which is really two adjectives; and I was pleased with myself for coming up with "sinful") when we started to hear yelling and hubbub coming from the window we'd vacated, as well as from the building across the way.

We knew we'd been caught. With no other choices, we made our way back to the open window. Diany was waiting inside, her face a mottled shade of red.

"What have you done, you crazy children! You could have fallen to your deaths!"

This sounded rather dramatic to me, though it was, in fact, what I had secretly thought to myself the first time we tried it.

"Not only that, but now we are at risk of being kicked out of the building!" She was shaking. I couldn't tell if it was out of anger at our disobedience, fear for our safety, or quite possibly as a result of having been yelled at by either Mummy or the building manager.

Apparently, the apartment complex manager had received complaints from flabbergasted onlookers and had phoned Hoop, who was enjoying tea in a neighboring building, as was her routine that day. He told her the family would have to leave if ever we children were to do such a thing again. She immediately phoned Diany, who came running to find us. The yelling from across the way had been neighbors, either pleading for our safe return or demanding a strict punishment for us. It was hard to tell from such a distance.

I can tell you, Mummy and Daddy were very upset after this. Even Daddy, who usually had an even temper and was often whistling and smiling and relaxed when he wasn't in meetings or arguing with Mummy, seemed less tolerant of us over the next couple of weeks. And dear Diany, she took the brunt of it all, I'm afraid, for it had been, after all, her responsibility to keep an eye on us while Mummy and Daddy were out.

Of course, we were expressly forbidden to go out on the ledge any more, and that certainly limited our ability to explore. Because have I even mentioned the elevator?

Chapter Five – Going Up

Living in an eight-story building had its advantages and disadvantages. I, for one, enjoyed a view, and so being up high was loads of fun, especially when sending paper airplanes out a window or bird-watching. Up so high, I feltv like a king on a mountain.

Of course, with all those stairs, the Residence Palace had an elevator—a small metal cage that worked by way of pulleys to magically bring you up or down without all that wear and tear on your legs and feet and knees.

However, there were elevator rules. And one rule was that no one under the age of sixteen was allowed to use the elevator without the supervision of someone older. Sis was only ten years old when we came to the Residence Palace, and I was six, with Jim Bill in the middle at nine.

The building manager and our parents and Diany were quite firm on this count, but we didn't often let rules stop us, as may seem apparent. We felt we had an eternity before us until Sis would be old enough to take Jim Bill and I up and down. Not using the elevator limited our activities somewhat, which is why we needed to find entertainment such as ledge-walking.

We often looked longingly at that elevator, imagining all the fun we could have if only we could travel up and down at will. Sometimes we just stared at the mesh cage in the middle of the stairwell and waited to see if it would head up or down. The cables that moved it were quite visible, and it made a creaking mechanical sound each time it lurched into operation.

Of course, if we went somewhere with Diany or our parents we rode on the elevator, but this was not necessarily a daily occurrence.

Sometimes on the weekend, Huck would take us to the Parc Cinquantenaire. We could look up at the trees, climb the smaller ones with lower branches, and walk along with Huck admiring the architecture and watching the other park goers. We sometimes brought balls to toss or to kick and chase through the park grounds.

Other favorite excursions took us to nearby Parc du Tervuren or the Au Beau Soleil swimming pool.

During the week, however, when everyone was busy, we had to create other amusements, one of which included standing on the landing of our floor and spitting into the elevator shaft.

Jimmy was quite good at it, spitting far further than Sis or I. We had a habit of letting the saliva hang in long droplets from our mouths and waiting til they fell of their own accord, whereas Jimmy would vigorously hurl his spitballs. Soon, our mouths would get dry and we'd become tired of the whole thing. Besides, Mummy and the concierge did not approve of this type of fun at all. It often turned out to be Jimmy who had the best ideas, so he sometimes caught a little more of the aftermath than Annie or I did.

Jim Bill has always been my favorite person on the planet, my partner in crime and comrade in arms. I could rarely turn him down when he had a great idea, even though sometimes, his great ideas got us in trouble.

Sometimes we would get a talking to, other times a *loud* talking to, and then there were times when plans simply didn't go as expected.

If truth be told, there were times we kids got to feeling a little like criminals. Daddy and Mummy's reactions to our periodic "adventures" seemed to be getting more intense and severe. Daddy's patience had started wearing thinner and thinner as the months had gone on. The arguments between he and Mummy had almost stopped, but now there seemed instead to be a cold wall between them.

Sometimes I caught Daddy glaring at Mummy, but that was only if they were in the same room, which was not often. Huck still gave us hugs and asked about our days, but he seemed to be present only in body. Sometimes when we talked to him, he only nodded and said, "Ah, yes, well then" when it wasn't really called for.

Annie seemed more affected by all of it than Jimmy and I. She developed a crinkly line between her eyes that appeared whenever we were scolded, or worse, when no one seemed to notice something we'd done—good or bad.

Sometimes Annie would shake her head if Jimmy and I tried to start a game or suggest an adventure. I supposed she didn't want to get in trouble. It wasn't as much fun without Annie, but Jimmy and I usually had more than enough fun plans, whether she was interested in participating or not.

One day, Jimmy and I climbed down all the stairs to the lobby and played a rousing game of hide and seek. The game made us quite warm and sweaty, and the prospect of walking back up all the stairs to our apartment seemed more than either of us could commit to.

The next thing I knew, Jimmy was walking towards the elevator. There was no one else about, and Jimmy stood with his fists on his hips, just staring. I saw a telltale look of determination on his face, and then the smallest hint of a smile on just one side of his mouth.

He turned his head and looked at me with a sly smile. "I have an idea," he said. "Look here, Broy. What if I rode not *in* the elevator, but *on* it?"

He looked quite pleased with himself as the words came out of his mouth, almost as if they'd been a surprise even to him.

"How?" was all I could manage, both skeptical and starting to get goose bumps.

"Look there," he said, pointing. I followed his finger to the top of the elevator car. "I can just go up the stairs part of the way, then climb up on top of the elevator and you can push the button! Then off I'll go, like gangbusters!"

I smiled in spite of myself; we both knew it would be more like a stroll in the park than a powerful locomotive. The elevator was slow and plodding. Faster than walking up stairs, I'll grant you, but not exactly a thrill in speed.

Jimmy knew he had my support before I even agreed. He began up the wide stairs next to the cage and hoisted himself up like a monkey onto the top of the elevator car. He peeked down at me through the gap while his feet dangled off the edge of one side.

"On my count, Broy! Push the button when I get to three!"

"Wait! Wait!" I sputtered. "Which number shall I push?"

Jimmy took a moment to think this through. I could almost hear his wheels turning. But we also both felt a sense of urgency, knowing that at any moment, either the concierge or another resident could walk in.

"Well," began Jimmy, "I don't think you should press the eight. I don't know how much room is at the top when you get there. So let's shoot for seven, okay?"

His logic could not be argued with, and seven seemed a far luckier number, in any case.

I stepped gingerly toward the elevator.

"Okay, on my count!" he yelled. "One....two....three!"

I paused, my finger hovering over the small round button with the "7" standing out, gold against the black surface. Taking a deep breath, I pushed it and jumped back from the car.

Then four things happened all at the exact same moment: the elevator lurched to life; Jimmy let out a scream; Daddy and another man walked in; and Daddy ordered me to stop the lift immediately, which I did, pressing the Stop button with force.

Daddy yelled, "Jim, what are you doing up there?! Get down at once!"

Jimmy came shimmying off the top of the elevator cage back onto the stairs, faster than I would have believed possible, and began bolting up the stairs. Daddy could be a little scary on the rare occasions he was angry.

Daddy barreled after Jimmy, two steps at a time. I followed behind, scampering to keep up. By the time we caught up to Jimmy, he had made it up an entire flight of stairs and was lying on the first landing, wincing in pain. His ankle was the size of a honeydew melon. "I can't walk, Daddy," Jimmy said, his voice ragged with misery. "It hurts."

Daddy's face lost its angry mask, and instead grew worried and tender. He pushed the button for the elevator, lifted Jimmy gently into his arms, brought him to our apartment, and phoned for a doctor. As Jimmy lay on the sofa with a pale face, I watched in fascination.

"Jimmy, how did you run up a flight of stairs if you were in so much pain?" I asked, quite impressed, even in the midst of all his obvious discomfort.

Jimmy took a sharp breath, then said, "I was scared of Daddy. I didn't even feel it right away."

After the elevator incident came a period of abject suffering where we had to endure a stern talking to, stricter rules on what games we could play, and further distance, it seemed, between Daddy and Mummy. The one silver lining was that Annie, feeling sorry for Jimmy and his painful ankle, rejoined our ranks to a degree, though she would not agree to anything she deemed remotely dangerous.

Jimmy's ankle, as it turned out, had been snapped by a metal bar that was part of the elevator shaft when his foot had been hanging off the side of the elevator cage. He ended up with a cast that went straight up to his knee and he had to wear it for a long, long time. When it was removed months later, his leg had grown so skinny and pale, and the flesh had become so dry and flaky, I nearly fainted. But before that happened, we had to survive the "invalid" time.

During the first two weeks he nearly died of boredom in bed, unable to put weight on his ankle at all. After that, Jimmy was able to walk on it, but clumped about like a lamb with its hoof caught in a bucket. You could hear him coming forever before he reached you, thump-thump-thumping down the hallway. Sis and I thought it quite funny, and we spared no time in finding ways to torment poor Jim Bill.

—

Chapter Six – An Education

Before I could read, I began to feel ever-so-slightly frustrated. I knew there was a world of adventure and information locked away in the covers of books, a world whose code I could not decipher. When I first started learning letters and their sounds, I was sure it was only a matter of time before the doors of imagination and knowledge would open wide for me. But those doors were slow in opening, one small crack at a time, one word at a time.

Once, when Annie had injured her eye in a game of tug-of-war, I became her nurse and personal attendant. The cornea of her eye had been scratched, and she had to keep it covered.

I told her I would read her a story, and got a book. But try as I might, I just didn't know all the words. Annie, ever the helper, simply asked me to spell the words I didn't know and then told me what they were. It worked, albeit slowly. Annie never got cross or impatient with me, and so I felt I was being useful rather than causing her strain.

Our love of books started early. Back when we were very little, and Huck and Hoop would read to us from children's books, we knew every story by heart and sometimes would act out the stories. Jimmy was usually the antagonist.

He liked to trick us or chase us or pretend to eat us. This was his favorite role, and sometimes at night he would slip back into his character without telling us. Before you knew it, a fox was chasing you down the hall, or a hare was racing you (Jimmy liked to run), though he might suddenly throw himself in front of you while you ran, so that you'd trip or stumble.

For many months after Jimmy's experiment with riding atop the elevator, running was out for him, as was going up and down the stairs, riding his bike, and jumping up and down on the beds. Reading, once again, took him, and all of us, on adventures and journeys in our minds. Huck had an extensive library, so we could often be found there, looking for titles that interested us. Of course, not all the books in Huck's library were stories.

We discovered the *Encyclopedia of Sexual Knowledge* on a top shelf, inconspicuously standing alongside other tomes. We quickly discovered it wasn't a story, so much as research and instruction. But it did have pictures...of *anatomy*. And when we read what the pictures were of, we could barely suppress our giggles. It was hard to imagine either Huck or Hoop reading it.

One morning after breakfast, Annie and I pulled the book out of its usual location to continue our education. We read only when Hoop and Huck were away, which was a good part of the day, and when Diany was not about. So far, we'd had several "lessons" over a period of about two weeks.

That particular morning, Hoop and Huck were both out and Diany was busy cleaning up from breakfast. Annie and I entered the study, shut the door quietly, and removed the book from the shelf. We sat on the window seat and opened to Book 3, "Sexual Organs in Function."

We had already read Books 1 and 2 ("Sexual Art of Primitive and Other Races," and "The Road to a Full Sex Life," respectively). Both had proven to be full of facts, some more interesting than others. We were trying our best not to look ahead to Book 10, "Delaying Sexual Death."

"Ahem, let us now begin," Sis began, in her most professor-like voice. She pushed her imaginary glasses up her nose. "Are you taking notes, Beverly?"

I smirked and took out my imaginary pencil and tablet, pencil poised to jot down pertinent information. I sat up straight and looked alert.

Just then Jimmy came in, noisily throwing open the door and thumping and bumping along in his knee-high leg cast. "What are you reading?" he asked. He had the decency to shut the door behind him.

Sis ignored him and continued, "Please make sure to take legible notes, Beverly. We will need to review them later as the pictures in this book are so distracting that we may well forget every word we read."

"Say," said Jimmy, "is that the *Encyclopedia* again?"

Just then Annie looked up, smiled in a most sinister way, then fell out of character and started laughing, turning the book towards me so that I could see the pictures. I was shocked to see a very large male organ, and burst out laughing as I felt my cheeks redden.

"Let me see!" Jimmy called as he hobbled towards us.

As he approached, Sis and I jumped up from the window seat and tore past Jimmy, Sis with book in hand.

"Jimmy," Sis said tauntingly, "these pictures aren't appropriate for you. And besides, you haven't attended all my lectures." Annie could be quite mean when she wanted to.

Jimmy hobbled as fast as he could in our direction, a furrow in his brow and a steely look in his eyes. "Let me see that!" he yelled, thumping emphatically.

Sis and I scurried back across the room, starting to breathe more heavily. My heart was pumping hard. I knew if Jimmy caught me, he might use that cast to kick me in the shins.

"What's the matter Jimmy?" Sis teased. "You seem to be having some difficulty reaching your destination. What is it you want?" She offered him the book, stretching her arms out. "Is it this? This old book?"

Jimmy rounded on us both and moved at a speed we didn't think he was capable of, his arms pumping as he gained momentum. This time Sis split off to his right, while I veered to his left. He reached out and grabbed part of my shirt sleeve and I yelped. Pulling away with some difficulty, I leapt onto a chair. I felt a little nervous, to be honest. Jimmy seemed fairly upset.

"Let me see that book!" he demanded, and took off after Annie. He was gaining on her, and for the first time, I felt he might actually catch her. When Jimmy was determined, he could be quite aggressive, and it seemed he didn't realize he had a cast on his foot or was aware it should be hindering him.

At this point, Annie was holding the book high above her head. She was a good five inches taller than Jimmy, so it seemed plausible it might be out of reach. As Jimmy got within arm's reach, I covered my face and jumped up and down in excitement (and I'll admit, a little fear). Just then, the door handle began to jiggle.

We all froze.

We heard someone coughing and clearing their throat, and watched as the door handle turned and seemed to get stuck. Realizing it must be Diany, we wondered at the unusual amount of trouble she seemed to be having opening the door.

Sis quickly slipped the book under a pillow. We three became co-conspirators, working together. Jimmy motioned for me to get down off the chair as he and Annie sat promptly on the sofa, trying to appear relaxed. I hopped down so quickly that the rough material of the chair rubbed the skin on the backs of my legs. I wondered if there would be a red mark later.

Diany entered the room, looking down at the floor, then slowly looked up with an innocent smile on her face.

"And what are you children up to this morning?" she asked, as if she didn't have an inkling.

Sis was sitting with her back against the pillow that hid the book, and had her hands clasped in her lap perhaps a little too tightly.

"We're just...discussing our plans for the day," Sis said, turning to Jimmy for affirmation.

"Yes, that's what we're doing," he said, nodding his head.

"Oh, and what are your plans, then, my dears?" she asked.

"I should think we might read," Annie offered, gesturing to the many books on the shelves.

"Anything in particular?" Diany asked.

Jimmy stood and began browsing the titles. He randomly picked a book off the shelf and started paging through it.

"Perhaps this..." he said, appearing to get lost in the fascinating text.

Diany smiled sweetly. "What a lovely idea! And I shall just straighten up in here. Those pillows need straightening," she said as she approached Annie's position on the sofa.

"Oh Diany, you work so hard," Annie began hastily. "Why don't you relax this morning? We kids don't do nearly enough around here to help. We'll straighten up, and even dust the bookshelves." Annie was not giving an inch on the sofa, and had entrenched her body deeper into the pillow and sofa, securing the book's hiding place.

I hopped up immediately and began brushing imaginary dust and debris from the chair I'd only just been standing on.

"Are you sure?" asked Diany.

We all said "yes" in unison.

"Well," Diany said, "do remember to put back any books you may take out." She looked directly at Annie, whose face was looking a little peaked. "You know how your dear father likes his study to look. I don't suppose he'd want to discover any books missing or out of place." At this she smiled, and turned to leave.

Chapter Seven – Farewells

In 1938, I had my best birthday yet. It wasn't because of presents or being the center of attention. It was because that year, the O'Learys came to visit. Hoop's sister, Aunt Anna O'Leary, and her husband, Uncle John O'Leary, traveled to Brussels. Even more exciting, they brought our Cousin Bonnie.

Bonnie was a fun, kind, and positive person. But even more importantly, she was sixteen; we could finally ride the elevator whenever we pleased. Sis, Jimmy, and I had all been looking forward to their visit, and were even considering showing Bonnie the *Encyclopedia*. Annie said if we did, though, we would have to pretend that nothing in it shocked us, so as not to appear babyish to Bonnie.

Bonnie ferried us up and down on the elevator to our hearts' content. Jimmy was out of his cast by this time, and able to join us on jaunts to the park and keep up with us on our travels.

While the O'Learys were with us, we visited Paris, Holland, and Germany, to name a few. Though many of the places and sights we saw were ones we'd seen before, it somehow seemed, with Bonnie there, that we were seeing them for the first time.

At the Eiffel Tower, we posed for pictures over and over again, smiling, making faces, and all as if we'd never done exactly that in times past.

It was in Paris that Huck first demonstrated the fine art of using chopsticks, where we practiced picking up almonds at a Chinese restaurant.

In Germany, we traveled to the Rhine River and the Black Forest. Uncle John showed us a battlefield he'd actually fought on during World War I.

"You see that barn there?" Uncle John asked as we stood on the former battlefield. He was pointing to a slightly dilapidated wooden structure just off the road. "I had to hide in there for three days, never making a sound." Our eyes were trained on him, waiting.

"My buddies and me, we knew there were Germans out there and we knew if they heard even a rustle, we'd be dead."

"You mean killed?" Jimmy asked. His eyes were bright and he sounded excited.

"Yes, Jimmy. We were the enemy. It was their job to make sure none of us made it out alive!"

"But you must have come out eventually! How did you get away?" Jimmy asked, almost impatient for the conclusion.

"Now Jimmy, give Uncle John a chance to finish and catch his breath," implored Daddy, familiar with Jimmy's tendency towards over-eagerness and excitability.

Uncle John looked hesitant, but then continued.

"We were out of food and water, and we knew we had two choices. Stay in the barn and die of starvation, or leave the barn and face the Krauts."

My stomach rumbled just then, and I wondered how long I could go without eating. Not very, it would seem.

"We decided to take our chances, figuring if we stayed, we were dead for sure, but if we left, we had a fighting chance."

At this, Uncle John motioned for us to follow him as he approached the barn. We stepped onto the dry, prickly grass and crossed an expanse of open land, the same open, unprotected space Uncle John and the other soldiers had to cross from the relative protection of the barn. I suddenly felt exposed.

Uncle John reached the barn first, and studied the face of the building for a few moments before continuing.

"Ah! Here...take a look at this."

We all gathered in closer and followed where his hands were touching the slightly rotting wood. Dark smudges of black with holes through their centers marred the surface.

"Are those from bullets?" Jimmy practically shouted.

"That's right," answered Uncle John. "But before any shooting happened, we had to get up the nerve to leave. I remember I looked at my buddy, Frank. He had dirt all over his face and his lips were cracked and bloody. We just stared at each other. We knew what we were up against, but we also knew we had no choice. 'You ready?' I asked him. He gave a slight nod and stuck his chin out. I knew he was determined. But I also knew he was scared. But nobody said they were scared. That's not what soldiers do." And here, Uncle John stopped for a minute, lost in his memories.

But Jimmy had no patience for nostalgia. "So what happened? Who shot who? Did you kill any Krauts?"

Uncle John looked at Jimmy and took on a very serious tone.

"Jimmy, I know it sounds exciting, and I suppose it seems that way even to soldiers before they have to face the reality. But I can't say now that it was exciting. We did what we had to do to survive. That's what soldiers do."

"But what happened?" Jimmy persisted. I could see that despite his love and respect for Uncle John, there was potential for an angry outburst if he didn't get the story he felt was due.

Uncle John took a deep breath and let it out slowly.

"All right Jimmy, girls. I'll tell you what happened. But remember, these were different times.

"Frank and me and the other boys, we gave each other the signal to start to head out. We crawled slowly towards the doorway, stopping every few feet to listen. There could've been enemy soldiers right outside the door, or in the woods in the distance. We didn't know. One of the other guys, I don't remember his name, he lay as low as he could on the ground and slowly peeked around the edge of the door frame. We held our breath, not sure what to expect, but ready with our Springfields—those are rifles."

Jimmy's mouth opened a little but he didn't interrupt.

"When nothing happened, the guy gave us the go signal, and we all slowly advanced on our bellies, rifles at the ready. There was so much open land, which made us easy targets, but we'd made our decision.

"Once outside, we kept inching forwards, see?" And Uncle John, though he didn't get down on his belly, did start slowly moving away from the barn.

"It was quiet outside. Not a sound. At first this seemed good. We thought we might even have gotten lucky. But then, maybe too late, we realized it was too quiet. There should have been birds or cows or something. But there wasn't even a barking dog.

"We were about 20 feet out from the barn and starting to rise up off our bellies onto our hands and knees when we heard it."

"What? Heard what, Uncle John?" Jimmy spoke for all of us at this point.

"It was a sound I hope I never hear again," Uncle John confided, and for a moment, he actually looked paler.

"'*Feuer Frei*!' That means fire at will! And the next minute, the air was full of the sound of gunshots! We scrambled back towards the barn, the only place there was for cover. Bullets ripped through the wood like it was paper!" And here, Uncle John pointed to the bullet holes again. He ran into the barn, us close behind.

"It wasn't much cover, but at least they didn't have a visual on us any more. We each cocked our rifles and prepared for battle. We knew we didn't have much time."

"Did the Germans come for you? Did you hide?" Jimmy seemed frantic to get the answers, and though I didn't voice it, I felt the same. What happened? How had he escaped?

"Hiding was pointless, Jim," Uncle John continued. "They knew where we were, even knew how many of us there were. But that's when I realized something important, probably the realization that saved my life."

We all held our breaths. Even Daddy.

"One thing you learn in combat is what the different sounds of gunfire mean. The Germans had machine guns and tanks, but also rifles, not unlike our own. And one thing was clear...this was not machine gun fire."

We all stood still, unsure of the significance of this fact.

"You see," continued Uncle John, "if it were machine gun fire, that meant that the Germans could shoot from quite a distance, very rapidly, and we probably wouldn't be much of a match. But if they had rifles like we did, well, we were at least given a fighting chance. In those few seconds, I also realized that the gunshots had come from one direction only, a tree line a few hundred meters from the barn, which meant the Germans hadn't surrounded us. Perhaps they were a small group as well. There was a chance we were evenly matched, which meant there was a chance we would survive.

"We formed a quick plan, all the while, lying low, with occasional gunfire bursting towards us. It seemed the enemy was tentatively shooting, but not advancing, a further clue that there weren't many of them. We knew we couldn't stay indefinitely in the barn. We knew that turning our backs on them meant sure death. The only other option was to run out of the barn as fast as we could directly towards the gunfire in the hopes of surprising the Germans."

Annie looked skeptical and concerned and scared, all at once. "But...but Uncle John, that seems like a sure way to be hit..."

"I don't disagree, Annie. But understand, we were faced with few options, and this was the only one where we even had a chance.

"I raised my hand like this," and Uncle John lifted his arm, his hand looking like it was ready to chop the air.

"On the count of three, we would rush the Germans, firing at them as we ran. One...two..."

At this, I moved closer to Daddy, taking hold of his arm.

"Three!" Uncle John's hand came down and he dashed out of the barn. We had no choice but to follow.

"We ran towards the gunfire, yelling and shooting. I don't remember that we planned to yell, but it just burst out of each of us, to a man! It must have been terrifying! I felt like a power other than my own had taken control and was propelling me forward."

"Then what? Then what?" Jimmy yelled.

"We didn't all make it to the tree line where the Germans had formed," Uncle John said, his voice faltering a little. "But many of us did, and the looks on their faces were of sheer surprised terror. Some of them ran, some dropped their weapons and surrendered. But really, once you get that close, guns almost aren't any good. We rushed into them, knocking some of them down and literally scrapped around on the ground, throwing punches and kicking."

"Wow!" Jimmy shouted excitedly. "Wow!" And he began kicking the air and throwing punches at imaginary foes. "Take that!" he yelled, fire in his eyes.

"In the end," Uncle John whispered, "it was us or them. I'm not proud of taking another man's life, but when it comes down to it, you find sometimes that your instincts take control, and if you're in fear for your own life, you'll do anything...anything to survive."

Uncle John's voice trailed off and he walked slowly back towards the road.

"But wait!" Jimmy cried. "Was there blood? How many did you kill?"

"That's enough Jim," Daddy said, placing a heavy hand on Jimmy's shoulder. "That's enough."

* * * * *

After two weeks of visiting and adventures, time began to speed up and we knew that all too soon, the O'Learys would need to return to America, and Bonnie to her school. However, her parents and Hoop and Huck decided it would be good for Bonnie to return to Belgium in the spring for her last term. She would attend the Belgian school to improve her French. We three kids already spoke French all the time to Diany and were quite fluent. And we knew that when Bonnie came, we would be able to converse with her, and maybe even teach *her* some words.

We had made oodles of new friends and practically became native speakers when we moved from our American school to the Belgian school, Cours d'education Carter. This had been precipitated after Jimmy had gotten kicked out of yet another school. Daddy said the Belgian teachers would be better at challenging Jimmy than the American school teachers had been, so that he didn't get any naughty ideas of what to do with idle time.

* * * * *

In February 1938, Mummy boarded a ship for New York. It seemed as if all the fun suddenly dried up. January, so full of hope and promise with the new year, was over. My birthday had come and gone, the O'Learys had left, and the weather was gray and dull. Mummy's departure felt like one more ending.

Just before she left, she sat us down to remind us of her reasons for going to America. She told us again about the dentists and her neuralgia, and added that her paperwork was all in order. She assured us, again, that the time would pass quickly and she'd return to us soon.

However, in early March when Annie received her first letter from Mummy, it seemed her original plans had changed.

Annie read the letter to herself. Her face became quite still as she neared the end.

"What's it say?" Jimmy and I asked together.

"Well," Annie said, "Mummy's teeth are feeling better. But it doesn't appear Mummy will be coming back just yet. She is going to surprise Grandmother for her birthday, and try to convince her to travel to Florida on a vacation."

Jimmy and I sat quietly for a moment. I suddenly wished Bonnie, Aunt Anna and Uncle John were still here. Our house seemed quite empty. I knew what Bonnie would say about Mummy's letter. She'd say, "Well isn't that lovely! I'm sure your grandmother will love a visit from her!" For she was very cheerful and positive at all times, and in that moment, I desperately missed that positivity. I tried to do a "chin up" and pretend this was great news.

"What else does it say?" Jimmy asked.

"Mummy is hoping Christianity will save us from another world war," Annie said, somewhat sarcastically.

"What's that supposed to mean?" Jimmy asked. He seemed angry with Annie.

"She says here, 'If the world and its leaders will try Christianity everything will come right very quickly and we can avoid another big world war.'"

"Are we going to have another world war?" I asked. I tried to picture soldiers hiding in barns and having to fight hand-to-hand with their enemies as Uncle John had done. But no one answered me. So I pretended Bonnie was sitting next to me, and she smiled and put her arm around me.

I imagined her saying, "Your father will never let anything bad happen to you Dearsie! You needn't worry. If there is another war, I have no doubt that we shall be on the right side of it and prevail!" That is what Bonnie would say.

But really, what was being said right then was this:

"And just how is Mummy going to persuade all the world to try Christianity, then?" Jimmy asked, sounding unconvinced that all was right with the world, and getting louder by degrees.

Annie looked like she was going to say something, then stopped. She picked the letter up again and said, "Well, Mummy does have some very influential friends. She is going to visit her friend Margaret

Woodrow Wilson, the former President's daughter. She seems to think Miss Wilson will be able to do something about it."

Although I was still quite young, something told me it would take more than two determined women to stop a war from starting.

*   *   *   *   *

We were quickly distracted when our next visitor, Aunt Bernice, arrived. She was Daddy's younger sister, and we adored her. She brought us dresses from Sears Roebuck that we had chosen out of a catalog. She gave lots of hugs, which we ate up like candy. She was sweet and kind, and almost never seemed cross or upset.

However, when we were discussing which countries to visit with her, she told Huck she was quite happy to tour the French Riviera, Avignon, and Italy. But she refused to set foot in Germany.

I remembered Germany as quite a beautiful country. Our trip there with Uncle John, Aunt Anna and Bonnie had been memorable; the people were nice, and the food was delicious. But Aunt Bernice got a dark look on her face when we brought it up, looking at Daddy and pursing her lips while shaking her head just a little.

"You won't get me on THAT country's soil, Charles," she said.

We asked her why, but she would only say what they were doing wasn't right and she didn't agree with their politics.

Still, we managed a fine time without Germany, revisiting favorite stomping grounds we'd seen with the O'Learys and finding new favorites, including a small open-air market in Paris with the fluffiest, most light and buttery croissants any of us had ever had. Aunt Bernice was a warm and loving presence, but her visit came to an end as well, eventually.

When Aunt Anna and Bonnie returned in April of 1938 after Bonnie's spring break, we couldn't have been more relieved and excited to have them back. Our apartment seemed less empty with Aunt Anna cooking special meals and Bonnie keeping everyone's spirits up. Jimmy had a little crush on Bonnie, so behaved most unlike himself when she was around.

Annie and I giggled every time Jimmy would bring Bonnie a napkin or open a door for her. He was ten years old, but trying to pretend to be sixteen, like Bonnie. His attempts to sound intelligent and mature whenever he'd speak around her had us in stitches. But he was still Jim Bill at heart, and still made faces at Sis and me when Bonnie wasn't looking.

In the months that followed, we continued our studies but looked forward to summer break. Bonnie's French became more fluent every day and we all spoke French much of the time. Diany teased us sometimes about our pronunciation, saying we sounded as though we were trying too hard...which I didn't understand, because shouldn't you always strive to do your best?

All too quickly, the spring term ended and our family shrank back down to just we three kids, Diany, and Daddy. Daddy missed his conversations with Aunt Anna, which must have been an extra treat since they could have "adult" discussions. Letters from Mummy came in sparse supply, some from Florida where she recounted her travels with "Miss Rose," the grandmother we'd never met. The distance felt more than geographical.

CHAPTER EIGHT – THE FALL

After Bonnie and Anna returned to America, it was summer. We three stretched our legs and imaginations as the days lengthened. Annie, almost twelve, was starting to spend less time playing games with Jimmy and me, and more time reading and staring at herself in the mirror. Still, we all got on quite well.

When we all got the chicken pox, Annie continued in her role as nursemaid, dabbing each of our blisters with calamine lotion. When Jimmy had his tonsils out, Annie and I pretended to be both doctor and his nurse, taking his temperature, checking his pulse, and prescribing all manner of imaginary medications and salves to speed up his recovery.

Jimmy was none too happy about being laid up yet again: first his broken ankle, then his tonsils. He said if one is going to live a full life, one must take risks, sometimes resulting in injury, or even death!

While Jimmy said he hated being sick, I wondered how much, what with all the cool drinks and ice cream he got, and all the doting from Diany, Sis and I. I wasn't jealous, but I did think he rather liked it more than he admitted.

I wondered if Mummy, with all the dental work she'd had done, might have been relegated to eating only ice cream. We hadn't heard much about her teeth, but we had a telegram from her that said she might become an Ambassador to Russia. President Roosevelt was making progressive changes during his administration, one of which included Secretary of State Cordell Hull considering the very first woman ambassador. Mummy, through her many political connections (she was good friends with Margaret Wilson, and had many friends and acquaintances through her years at Daddy's side, some of whom were now in Washington) had made that list.

I didn't know if this was good news or not. Maybe as the Ambassador, she could do what she'd said and bring Christianity to the other leaders and help stop the war. I supposed she would have to move to Russia and wondered if we would go there too. Would we need to learn to speak Russian? She herself was taking lessons, and boasting somewhat about her progress.

* * * * *

That fall of 1938, things seemed to get more serious around our house. Daddy had many late-night meetings and telephone calls for work. He spoke to Mummy sometimes too, behind closed doors. It was clear they were back to yelling and terse words. We hadn't seen Mummy for eight months and had only talked to her on the telephone a few times. Her letters were mostly about the politics she spoke of with her friends, her detailed list of reasons why she would make a good ambassador, the dental work she'd had done, or the health of her sister Golder and her mother, Miss Rose. She gave little indication of returning.

In August, we had received a note from Aunt Anna and Uncle John, suggesting Mummy stay in the States "until the political situation is settled." She was living with her sister Golder on Connecticut Avenue in Washington, DC, approximately 35 miles from Quantico, Virginia where Uncle John, Aunt Anna and Bonnie lived.

During that autumn, Annie began wearing her hair down more often than in braids and seemed to walk taller, taking more responsibility around the house. She became interested in the news, and would listen to BBC radio broadcasts reporting on Hitler, Germany, and subsequent world events.

When Prime Minister Chamberlain spoke after returning from talks with Hitler, waving what he claimed was the Munich Agreement, Annie became both riled and sarcastic, echoing our own father's opinions. The two leaders agreed and even signed papers stating they would *not* go to war with one another. We heard cheering and clapping on the radio, and were told to get a good night's sleep since we had nothing to worry about. But many more people agreed with Daddy and Sis, protesting in Trafalgar Square, believing that Hitler would not stay true to his word, and thinking Chamberlain naive or maybe even under Hitler's spell.

When our school pictures were taken that year, Annie referenced Chamberlain's speech on the back in a note to Aunt Golder, to whom she was sending the picture. She attempted to sound like an adult. Jimmy and I heard the BBC broadcasts too, but most of them were so serious and full of so much information, I rarely understood, and really didn't want to. I preferred the musical programs.

Germany didn't keep its promises of peace. We soon heard news of Germany occupying Sudetenland. Then came *Kristallnacht,* or "night of broken glass," where German mobs destroyed shops and synagogues all over Germany, breaking glass windows and burning buildings to the ground.

We heard of these things by listening to Daddy and Diany talking, by putting our ears to the door when Daddy was on the phone, and by our teachers at school whispering in the halls. Daddy no longer kept newspapers about, and limited our listening to BBC reports. He would never talk to us directly about any of what was going on. His face became more lined with wrinkles, and he didn't smile nearly as much as he used to.

Germany's destruction and violence seemed to be directed primarily against Jews, and was happening in other countries. So Daddy assured us we were still quite safe with him.

Mummy's letters seemed to stop, but we kids had become used to her absence and went about our lives, studying, shopping with Diany, and occasionally spending time with Daddy, though his job seemed to take up more and more of that precious commodity.

Daddy still got letters from Mummy, but didn't share them any more. Each time he read her small and compressed writing, he seemed at once both angry and weary, and required time alone for a bit before he was fit to be around. Diany felt the tension too, often watching him as he would leave or enter a room, seemingly holding her breath in anticipation of his possible foul moods. On these occasions, her dealings with we three kids was that of someone heavily distracted.

CHAPTER NINE – DECISIONS

It was the spring of 1939, and the warming weather put thoughts of summer playing in our heads. Jimmy was anxious to get outside and kick some balls and climb some trees. One Saturday, our spring fever prompted us to ask if we could go to the Parc.

"Perhaps later," Daddy said. He had a rather serious look on his face, which sadly had become the standard of late. "First, we need to talk about some things."

We suddenly lost our smiles and our energy, hearing the seriousness in his voice.

"You know that your mother has been working at becoming Ambassador to Russia. There may even be some people helping her to get that post. At first, I didn't—no one thought it possible. But I've come to realize she is determined and has many influential friends in Washington, DC." At this, he stopped. He steepled his hands, resting his chin on the tips, and looked into the distance.

"Children, I—" he stumbled over his words a bit, and we three shuffled in our seats uncomfortably. It didn't feel like good news was coming.

"Children, what I'm trying to say is, it's time we discussed, as a family, the possibility of—well, we need to talk about the idea of— what I mean to say is, I want to ask your thoughts on the idea of living there, with your mother. In Russia."

No one spoke at first. Daddy may as well have asked us our thoughts on living on the moon. Mummy had been gone for more than a year. She'd had all her dental work, but still wasn't back. She was having a good time with her mother and sisters, and her friends in Washington, so had extended her trip. Now, with all the talk of becoming an ambassador, she was staying close to Washington to see who the President would appoint.

There had never been a woman ambassador before, so Mummy's appointment as Russian Ambassador would be in all the news, and Mummy seemed almost driven to make this happen. Her Russian lessons, her many meetings with people she knew in Washington, and the pride that came across the ocean with her words were all indications that this would be a big accomplishment. A small part of me wanted to feel excited for her, but I couldn't summon any good cheer where her absence was concerned.

Daddy had a serious look on his face, but spoke softly and gently. Diany stood behind the couch, looking nervous. Maybe she was afraid we'd go and she would miss us terribly. Perhaps she would come with us.

"Children," Daddy said, "you have grown up so much and understand so many things. I felt it was time we had a real heart-to-heart."

Annie looked serious, her eyes not wavering, her arms stiff at her sides. Jimmy looked angry, his face a little twisted. He took a deep breath, controlled his features, and looked at Daddy. I dangled my feet and focused instead on whether there might be any chocolate left.

"Your mother may actually have the opportunity to serve as Ambassador to Russia. This is very important to her, and I think she means to go if the President asks." Diany bit her lip as Daddy spoke, her smooth cheeks pale and still.

"So," Daddy continued, "I wanted to discuss with you..." He shook his head quickly, then tried again. "What I mean to say is, it has been a very long time since you have seen your mother. She has told me...she has *asked* me to tell you that she should very much like you to come with her to Russia if, indeed, this appointment actually happens."

At this, Diany's face looked confused. "But I thought—"

At the same moment Jimmy started to say something, but Daddy stopped them both, his hand in the air to indicate he had the floor.

"Just a minute Diany, Jimmy, let me finish. I want you to have the facts so you can decide for yourselves. Your mother wanted to take Dearsie and Diany with her. But I would never consider separating you three."

At this, for the first time, I felt anguish and perhaps a little fear. It had never occurred to me that of all the options—Mummy coming home, we kids going to the States, or Mummy being appointed to

Russia— that the three of us kids would ever be anything but side by side by side. Daddy continued.

"If you really want to, we could figure out some way for you to be in Russia; but I have to warn you that your mother will be very busy with her new job, if—and this is a big *if*—she actually gets the appointment."

Daddy looked as if he had a bad stomachache. He winced a little. "If you decide you would rather spend some time with your mother, instead of staying here with me and continuing at school with your friends, you can, of course, decide to do that."

Daddy stopped and held his breath. He pinched the bridge of his nose. I wondered if he had a headache. Diany moved towards him looking as if she too was in pain, then stopped herself and held on to the back of the sofa.

I felt an uncomfortable feeling in my stomach. I didn't like serious talks, and this one was feeling like it might last longer than our usual scoldings or reminders. Jimmy fidgeted with his hands and looked like he wanted to say something but was trying to respect Daddy's request to wait. Annie was all ears and pursed lips.

"What I'm trying to say," Daddy said, his voice sounding almost like he'd swallowed too much honey, sort of sticky and thick, "is that I should be very sad and miss you so very much if you—any of you— went, but that I would never stop you if you would rather be with your mother."

At this, Daddy started to cough and rub his eyes. Diany looked miserable, her hands on her throat. Her face was pale, though a thin, red ring appeared around her forehead, as though she were exerting effort.

Annie, more animated, took a breath and said, "Oh Daddy, we should never want to leave your side!" And with that, she got up, ran over to him, and put her arms around his shoulders.

Jimmy finally blurted out, "We don't even speak Russian! Don't you want us to stay here with you?"

Daddy put a hand on Jimmy's shoulder and said, more quietly than before, "Of course I want you here. I shouldn't know what to do or how to begin without all of you near me."

A tear started in my eye. I felt confused, watching seemingly unspoken words passing between everyone.

Daddy looked over at me. "Dearsie, whatever is the matter? Come here my darling!" and he opened his arms. I didn't know I was crying, but apparently I was, and so I went to hide my face in his shoulder. His next words were closer, more resonant. I could hear them coming from his very depths: "Well, it's decided then," Daddy said with a huge sigh. "You shall stay here in Belgium with me and Diany!"

I looked up to see Diany standing just behind Daddy. Her eyes looked wet, but she was smiling.

* * * * *

Summer finally arrived. We traveled through Paris, Milan, and Switzerland as a getaway from the stress Daddy was under with work. He had just gotten a good report from Mr. Sussdorf, his boss, and wanted to celebrate with us.

Before we left, we overheard Daddy on the phone. It sounded as if someone were questioning his idea for the trip. He said, "Yes, I understand. But for now, Milan and Switzerland are quite safe and out of the fray. Yes, of course, we'll take every precaution. I just think they need a break from the tension. No, of course not. No, she doesn't know. Well, I hardly think it's her concern. Yes, I'll stay in touch. We should be back in a week or so."

On vacation, Daddy worked hard at relaxing. He proudly showed us the sights, encouraged our questions, took us walking and on picnics. He seemed to drink in the beauty of the landscape and look at us as though seeing us for the first time in a long while. Diany smiled and laughed a lot too, and we all forgot our cares, catching the contagious mood of joy.

Not long after we returned, Germany invaded Poland. It was in the news constantly, and Daddy became very concerned. At school, the teachers and students talked about it. When Germany started going into other people's countries the year before, it had seemed to be small news, but this apparently was BIG news. I don't understand how news gets to be big or small, only that when it's big, people talk about it a lot. One night after dinner, Annie and Jimmy were discussing it.

"I guess it's good we didn't go to Russia after all," Annie said.

"But Germany invaded Poland, not Russia!" I pointed out.

Jimmy took an impatient breath and said, "Yes, Small Stuff, that's true. But Germany and Russia are in cahoots together. They're dividing Poland like a pie. No wonder the President wouldn't let Mummy go to

Russia. He doesn't want anything to do with the Germans and their invasions."

We had learned Mummy's appointment had been denied. The President didn't feel a woman should be placed overseas during such trying times. I wondered if she felt disappointed, angry, or relieved. I imagined she was quite put out with the Germans right about then for keeping her from her post. From everything I overheard Daddy say to Diany, Mummy had been absolutely certain, and had been feeling excited about it. Mummy usually got her way, so this had probably upset her mightily.

Sometimes I tested myself to see if I could remember her face. I studied photographs that showed her classic beauty, her full, perfectly shaped lips, and her wide eyes. She sometimes reminded me of a statue in a museum. There was a picture of her taken when she was dressed as an Indian princess. It looked so dramatic. And another of her on the floor, arms stretched out, head lowered in supplication. She almost looked as though she had given over control.

But she must have been acting, because Mummy never gave in or gave up. When something didn't go her way, she didn't retreat into solitude; it was more like she retreated into a bear cave, waiting until the right time to come back out and attack. When she went to this place, she sometimes appeared quite distant and cold. We kids had always known not to disturb her when that faraway look came over her.

I began to wonder if her failed appointment would mean she would be returning to Belgium. I wasn't sure how I felt about that, but I was certainly curious to know. One night after dinner, I brought it up.

"So, now that Mummy isn't going to Russia, will she be returning home?" I asked.

Annie shot a quick glance at Jimmy, then said, "Well Bev, it's really not a good idea for anyone to travel right now. We shall stay put with Father right here, and she will stay put back in Virginia."

"But, if we aren't at war, and America isn't at war, why isn't it safe to go from one to the other?" I asked. This whole idea of war had become more than tiresome.

Jimmy looked at Annie and said, "Yes, what's the reason again?"

Annie smirked, then said, "It's just a precaution; no need to worry. We're quite fine here with Daddy, and here we shall stay. Daddy says no evacuations have been ordered, which is certainly a sign that staying in Belgium is the best plan for us."

Of course, the next thing you know, Mummy started trying to get us to do just the opposite.

CHAPTER TEN - THE LETTER

4700 Connecticut Avenue,
Washington, D.C.,
November 11, 1939.

Dearest Jim,

It was so good to hear the voices
of all of you yesterday.

When your birthday comes, I shall be
thinking of all of you and wondering what
you will be doing.

Ask Daddy to change this dollar into
Belgian money so that you can buy candy,
or something for a treat for you and
your sisters.

As for your coming over here; I hope
that Daddy will decide to send you at
once as everyone here thinks it would be
the safest. As for leaving Daddy, I am sure
that he will tell you that he would rather
have his children here with their mother
and in a safe country than over there in
danger and where you will soon be seeing
and hearing of the sick and dying soldiers.

You said yesterday that you did not know
that the war had started. I was very surprised that you did not know better than
that. The fighting has been going on over
there for over two months and may start in
Belgium at any moment.

2

Some parts of the ocean are mined as you said yesterday. However, Daddy could take you to Italy and put you on an Italian boat in charge of a stewardess and I will meet you in New york.

I have important friends who will ask the German, French, British and Italian governments to take special care of the boat that you sail on since you are children of an American official. And if Daddy will tell me whether he is going through France or Germany, I can get them to arrenge for safe conduct through the couhtry.

You see mama needs her boy to look after her for a while. Sons should look after their mothers. And I worry about you so especially since the war has started. So please tell Daddy to hurry and get you over here.

You asked about money. If Daddy has not got enough in his Belgian bank to pay your way, we hav about three thousand dollars invested through an office in London. He can get this quickly. And the safety of our three dear children is more important than any money we have.

When the war is over, I have enough to pay our way back to Belgium, and I will take you back myself.

Take care of your sisters on the boat and tell them not to try to walk about if the boat is rocking very much. I will see you when you step pff the boat in New York.

Much love to all, Mama.

Jimmy put the letter down.

"What does it say, Jimmy?" I asked.

Jimmy stood still for a few minutes. Then, he picked the letter back up and handed it to me.

"Here. Read it yourself. It is just more of the same." Jimmy went and pretended to flip through a book.

We had talked to Mummy on the phone a couple of weeks ago, and she had spent a lot of time talking to Jimmy about the war. She had said she wanted us to come to America. She believed it was safer than Belgium, and she had friends that could make sure we got there safely. But Jimmy hadn't fallen for any of that. Daddy had already filled him in on the dangers of the open sea, including mines and German submarines. And besides, there wasn't the money to pay our way, as ships were in great demand right now, so booking passage was expensive.

Daddy didn't let us stay on the phone for too long. When I had spoken to Mummy, she mostly told me I must be getting to be a big girl and she talked about her mother, Miss Rose, and how happy Miss Rose was to have her daughter back. I wanted to feel happy for Miss Rose and Mummy, but a piece of me felt something unusual; jealousy. Mummy was with her mother, and her mother wanted her around.

I read through Mummy's letter. It sounded a bit like she was asking for Jimmy to help keep *her* safe. But I knew that Hoop was the most resourceful woman in the world, and couldn't truly need the help of a 12-year-old boy. Maybe she was trying to make Jimmy feel good and build his confidence. But honestly, Jimmy's confidence had never been that much in need of boosting.

As to going to America, we three didn't want to leave Daddy behind in Brussels. Mummy had her sisters Golder and Anna, their children, and all her friends in Washington. She never seemed to be lonely or afraid.

Later, Annie read the letter too. Afterwards, she carefully folded it up, placing it back in the envelope. Her face was unreadable. She seemed to be preparing herself to respond in the most mature way possible, but having some type of internal argument.

Then she smiled at me, put on her gamest face, and said, "Let's go have a game of Bagatelle!"

I wanted to keep worrying about the letter, but Annie had pulled out her best trick. Bagatelle was our favorite game, and I could hardly resist.

I had gotten better at getting the metal balls into winning spaces, though sometimes I poked a ball too hard, sending it ricocheting off the sides of the board; not hard enough, and it went nowhere. Jimmy was best at it; Annie was fair, but not as good as Jimmy. I had a fair chance at victory.

CHAPTER ELEVEN – AND SO IT BEGINS

In the spring of 1940, Germany invaded Norway and then slowly started making its way into other countries such as Denmark, Holland, Romania, and Yugoslavia.

That was the first time I felt angry. Norway was a small country, very peaceful. I couldn't understand why Germany was being such a bully. Jimmy said that's exactly what it was, and that the German armies were starting to capture anyone who was Jewish and lock them up. This made no sense to me. How were Jewish people the enemy? Especially children! But that is what the rumors were starting to say.

When Russia, Germany's ally, invaded Finland, our cook was quite put out, and said that any Russian should be stripped and dressed in feathers because they were savages. Not for the first or last time, I was happy that Mummy didn't end up being Ambassador to Russia, and agreed with Daddy that we should not have gone there if she had.

We kids began to wonder if Belgium really was safe. When Poland had been invaded in September, a lot of Americans had headed back to the U.S. But Daddy's post remained intact, and so, therefore, had we. Most people believed Belgium would not be invaded.

At school, we were preparing for Mother's Day, a day when all children were supposed to give a gift to their mothers to show their love. I had spent the last couple of weeks of school sewing an apron for Hoop. Each time I pressed the needle through the fabric I felt its sharp point, and I often broke the thread by pulling too hard.

Before that, we had knit undershirts for the soldiers. I felt sorry for some of the soldiers, in part because I knew my finished shirt was probably not top-notch quality, nor as pleasant to look at as some of the undershirts the other girls made. But I imagined as long as it was warm and it fit, the soldier who received it wouldn't complain much.

As for the apron, well I couldn't in all honesty imagine Hoop ever wearing an apron, nor did I have any way to find out, as she was still tucked away in America, and I in Belgium where life continued to go on.

We practiced for the event of an air raid in our school, where we'd been issued gas masks and small leather identification tags. We had to copy out the rules for safety in case of an air raid, but I don't think anybody paid much attention to them. We were also instructed on where to go in case of an alert. One day, they told us we would have a drill the following Monday, but we never did. Most people still felt that Belgium would be spared in this war.

So while I worked on an apron that would never be worn, Sis was having a grand time in her class re-enacting the story of Hansel and Gretel as a Mother's Day play. Her teachers didn't approve of Germany, and had changed the names Hansel and Gretel to Poucet and Miquette. Annie said that even during her history lesson, when it came to learning about Germany, the teacher had quickly changed the subject, saying, "*Mais cela ne nous intéressé pas, n'est-ce pas?*" But that doesn't interest us, does it?

It was around this time that Huck got a new car, a Studebaker President. It was big and black, and he said we could ride in it just for fun. All of us were quite excited. If Mummy had seen it, she mightn't have approved; but then, maybe she would have. It was fancy and she might have been proud to be seen in it.

We were, all of us, busily thinking up all sorts of adventures we might have in the President. Picnics, outings, drives through the countryside with Jimmy running alongside, which had become his most recent way of releasing his energy. It was big and roomy and we all fit quite comfortably, including Diany. Daddy loved his new car and started to smile an awful lot more. Our smiles and laughs became contagious when we saw how Daddy felt about it.

At night, we went to bed dreaming of all the adventures we would have driving around the country in our luxurious President.

CHAPTER TWELVE – ADVENTURE SEEKERS

I woke to the light just starting to shine between the slats in my blinds. I generally like waking up, but on this morning I felt lazy, and shut my eyes again, trying to recapture my dreams, which were running away faster than butterflies from a net.

Jimmy was moving around, though, and so I guessed it was time to get up. Ever since Mummy had gone to America, Jimmy and I had been sleeping in her room. Annie still slept in her own room; after all, she was almost fourteen. But Jimmy and I liked sharing a room, whispering into the night, giggling and making up stories.

Although I was ten, I was still the youngest, and Daddy still called me Dearsie. It sounded like a name for someone quite a bit younger, but it also made me feel special, and I didn't mind sometimes if Daddy still wanted to treat me as though I was younger than I really was. Diany still liked to brush my hair, and Jimmy and Annie still bossed me around, so in many ways, I suppose I was still the baby of the family. But inside, I knew that no one meant to make me feel bad by it; it's just the way things were.

I rustled in my covers, unable to pretend to be asleep anymore. After all, the road workers were quite loud that morning. They had been doing road work on the Rue de la Loi for months, always pounding away with their picks and drills. It didn't bother me anymore, and I'd gotten used to the thought of them being there forever.

But as I became more awake, I began to realize the noises were not drills at all. In fact, the loud thumps and repetitive bursts sounded like what I thought must be guns. I had never heard guns before, but I didn't need a military expert to tell me that this was what I was hearing. And the other sound had to be canons.

"Jimmy, what's happening?" I asked, as I sat up in bed.

Jimmy was at the window peeking out.

"Anti-aircraft guns!" he said excitedly.

Annie came in just then, and we all huddled around the edges of the window. That's when we noticed another sound, a sinister, eerie wail that we recognized as the siren. We knew what it sounded like because they had sounded it one afternoon some time before to get the population accustomed to it. A lengthy series of low, moaning notes rose and fell, almost like a banshee, or a recording of a banshee that repeated in exactly the same rise and fall time after time.

We decided we had better go down to Daddy's room. We found Diany there, but she said Daddy was down in our end of the apartment, so back we tromped and found him in Mummy's room, where he had come looking for us. The four of us went over to the window and stood looking out. The sky was light blue, no clouds, quite lovely really. Then we saw the planes.

They appeared as distant silver specks high in the blue sky. We could hear the *a-aa-aa-a-aa-aa* of the tracer bullets, which looked like red balls from this distance.

"Gosh Pop, that's pretty!" we all chorused.

"It may be pretty, but the place for you is downstairs in the shelter," Daddy replied. Although the actual fighting was far away, Daddy thought it best we become familiar with the air raid shelters.

So we got on our slippers and dressing gowns and tramped to the back staircase and elevator. But the elevator wouldn't come up, so we made the trek down on foot. There were three basements in the Residence Palace. The shelter was on the first, just under the ground floor. We went to the door and tried it, but it was locked. Aside from some of our Jewish neighbors, we were the only ones there, it seemed no one else was taking the air raid too seriously.

When Mrs. Shultz found out the door was locked, she said, "*C'est scandaleuse, ça mais c'est scandaleuse!*" I saw her turn away to her husband, muttering over and over, "*scandaleuse, scandaleuse.*"

She and her husband followed us down to the third basement, where the janitor and his family lived. We asked for the key to the shelter, but the janitor's wife told us her husband had gone to get it. So we waited.

Even though we were down beneath the ground floor, we could still hear the booms and *rat-a-tats* from above. Annie clasped her hands together as she crouched in a doorway. She was muttering under her breath, but I could still hear her.

"Oh God, dear God, please," she kept repeating.

Daddy had his arm around me and I felt quite safe, knowing he wouldn't let anything happen to any of us.

At last the janitor came along in bedroom slippers and said the janitor of the other building didn't have the key, but had gone to get it from someone else. So we waited some more.

After some time, we received the news that no one could find the key to the shelter. We were told, however, if we went around to the other side of the building, we could go into the other shelter. Because the Residence Palace had four quarters, there were more shelters in the other buildings.

So around we went, leaving Diany behind to go upstairs and back to bed. She had not been feeling well lately, doing a lot of holding her stomach and wincing. Daddy said we could go back to bed too if any of us liked, since the actual fighting was so far away. But we rather liked the excitement of the search for shelter.

We went around to the other side of the building and found our way to the entrance of the old underground theater no longer in use, we found it locked as well. We sat on some benches to wait for a janitor. Every now and then, the ground shook and doors and windows trembled. Daddy kept his arm around me and Jimmy looking like a frozen statue. Mrs. Shultz stopped "*scandaleusing*" and looked right at me.

"If anyone tries to hurt you, I will not allow it! Do you hear me? You are safe, little one. I will defend you against them!" I looked at Daddy to see if this was an appropriate time to say "thank you," but he was not paying attention. He just kept staring ahead, gently rubbing my arm.

Daddy finally decided we should try back at the first shelter. The door was now mysteriously open; however, by now, the shooting had stopped. We still went in, just to check things out. It didn't seem any too special to me. The walls were made of concrete on three sides, and railroad ties on the fourth. Inside were a bunch of old mattresses. This seemed to please Daddy, however. I suppose if we needed to spend the night, they'd come in handy.

Once the sirens finally stopped, we made our way back upstairs, where we checked on Diany and had our breakfast. Daddy said, "Well, I don't suppose there's much chance of Belgium staying out of the war now. The janitor said the Germans have invaded Holland."

Daddy told us to start packing. He had been considering sending us to Dinard, near St. Malo, Brittany, but later decided to send us to Pilat-Plage near Arcachon, which was not far from Bordeaux, France.

He had wanted us to leave several days earlier, but then Diany became sick. Daddy had managed to get places for us on a train leaving for Paris the very next day. We were surprised, but nonetheless excited because traveling by train seemed so adventurous, and we loved a good adventure. To make things even better, we were going to travel with Dr. and Mrs. Spencer, who had been trying to get to Berlin where Dr. Spencer had a diplomatic post to fulfill. Due to the war, instead of heading directly northeast to Berlin, they were being forced to go south to the middle of France, then swing eastward through Northern Italy and up through Switzerland.

We quite liked the Spencers. Dr. Spencer was someone Daddy knew through his work, and he had recently wed his young pretty wife, Mrs. Spencer. The two held hands a lot and made eyes at one another. Annie and I giggled when this happened, but Jimmy usually looked towards the heavens and sighed heavily.

Diany seemed quite relieved that the Spencers would be coming with us. She had been increasingly nervous as news of the war became more and more alarming. Since she hadn't been feeling well, and we knew that packing everything and traveling would be stressful to her, we kids did our best to do our own packing and take responsibility for our own things, doing what we could to help dear Diany.

Chapter Thirteen – Departure

That night was full of excitement. During supper we had to go down to the shelter at least five different times because the siren kept going off. Then the all clear would sound, and back up the eight flights of stairs we would trudge. Then down again, and up again. We didn't finish supper till the next morning, after we'd spent the night on mattresses and folding beds in the shelter. Even something exciting, after it's been done over and over, can start to wear thin.

The sirens kept sounding all the next day as we prepared to leave for our 5:00 p.m. train. We grew quite confused, not knowing whether any given siren was saying "all clear" or what. Our leg muscles were aching like crazy and we were glad when it was finally time to depart because we didn't have to climb up all those stairs again.

News bulletins on the radio said all schools were closed till further notice. Then they seemed to be playing nothing but military marches, interspersed with the same song over and over: "We'll Hang Out Our Washing on the Siegfried Line." Jimmy tried to explain it to me, but I didn't understand completely. It had something to do with showing the Germans that their bullying wasn't working.

In the afternoon, a car arrived to get us. Poor Daddy said a quick goodbye to us, giving us brief hugs and telling us to be good and listen to the Spencers. He promised we would all be together again soon. He whispered something in Diany's ear that I couldn't quite hear. Her eyes looked red and swollen, as though she had been crying, and her face was pale. Perhaps she was still not feeling well.

As we left the Residence Palace to the sound of the sirens going off yet again, we all peered out the back window of the car, waving to Daddy and wishing he could come with us.

I overheard Mrs. Spencer whisper to Dr. Spencer, "Poor Mr. Broy's heart was in his mouth." Dr. Spencer saw that I was listening, and quickly smiled and started showering us with details of our trip and peppering us with all sorts of questions. Did we like to play cards?

Had we ever been to Paris? Did we suppose there would be any loud, annoying travelers on the train with us?

At the train station, people moved in erratic circles and seemed confused. Many of the travelers were children, like us. Some were scared and crying, but most looked excited. There was an air of nervous energy, the way one sometimes feels before playing a sport or going to a big party.

As the train departed from Brussels, an airplane accompanied us to the border between Belgium and France. I know it was supposed to make us feel safe, but the more I heard its drone and thought of its purpose, the less safe I felt.

Near the border, the train slowed to a snail's pace, and from time to time stopped altogether. Diany said they were being extra careful and cautious to make sure we arrived safely, but her hands were fidgeting and she kept peering about the cabin and out the train's windows and asking the Spencers what was happening.

The Spencers reassured us that all was well, though sometimes I saw Mrs. Spencer glance at Dr. Spencer, and she didn't look very sure of what she had been saying. I saw him pat her hand and give a little shake of his head, and once or twice, when Diany was peering out the window, they both looked at her, and then at each other, with frowns creasing their foreheads.

When we arrived at the French border the skies were black as ink, not a single light on outside. We were told to go inside the station to have our passports examined. However, there was a little bit of confusion as we left the car. Mrs. Spencer, who had packed quite a bit of luggage (fourteen pieces of hand luggage, to be exact, along with two trunks), seemed reluctant to leave it alone on the train.

"This is my trousseau and bridal linens! I am not risking losing them when I've labored so hard to bring them along!" she said to Dr. Spencer in a none-too-quiet whisper.

"Darling," he replied, not sounding all that gentle or loving at the moment, "we must get inside to safety."

"Safety? And just how is the station any safer than the train?" she shrilly argued.

"At least we'll be together," he urged, tugging on her arm. But she pulled her arm away and refused to budge.

"I will NOT abandon our luggage! I shall remain here and keep track of it." And she stood quite firmly.

Finally, he made her swear to take precautions.

"Darling," he pleaded, "you must promise me that you will remain on the floor of the train."

"Yes, yes, of course," she conceded, beginning to turn away from him.

"I'm not done yet," he continued. "You must lie on the floor with your mouth open. Do you understand? Leave your mouth open."

Mrs. Spencer started to question him, but he snapped, "We haven't got time for discussion! Will you promise me? Say it!"

Mrs. Spencer nodded, then whispered, "I will...I will."

Then Dr. Spencer, Diany, and we three were ushered into the large station, with its ceiling-high walls of glass. It was packed with people all waiting to have their passports checked. No sooner had we stepped inside than a soldier said something in a commanding voice and the lights in the station went out. There was complete silence for a few minutes, then the approaching drone of airplane engines. Everyone was terribly quiet. Just then, the rasp of a match sounded in the silence as someone lit a cigarette.

The soldier yelled, "*Eteignez! Eteignez! Ils vont nous voir!*" Put it out! Put it out! They will see us!

Everybody was shouting orders all at once. Then there was silence again, as a flashlight scanned the station. More orders were issued as the planes got closer.

This nerve-wracking volley of silence and orders continued as bombs fell in the distance. Each thud made each person minutely jump in their skin.

Annie was kneeling down and praying for protection. Diany was shivering and her teeth were chattering as though she was cold, though with all the people crammed in the station, it was quite warm. Dr. Spencer had his arms protectively over Jimmy and me, and he kept looking out towards the train. Twice during our ordeal, Dr. Spencer tried to get out, pleading with the soldiers that his wife was still on the train, but they would not let him leave.

Lights came on only briefly in the form of lanterns so that passports could be examined until the next time the lights would go out. I was quite tired of crouching down and not being able to really see anything or talk much.

67

At one point, Jimmy and I tried to play a miming game. One of us would silently act out an action while crouching, and the other would try to figure out what was being communicated. But our game was only half-hearted. We were really trying to pass the time, but everyone was so tense, and when the lights went out, you could barely see your own hand in front of your face, much less the hand of your brother.

After two and a half hours of planes, bombings, lights on and off, passport examinations, and soldiers' orders, we were finally allowed back onto the train. Dr. Spencer was visibly relieved as he reunited with Mrs. Spencer, who said she was fine. All their anger and annoyance seemed to have melted away. They hugged each other for a long while with their eyes closed.

Then Mrs. Spencer told us that a British troop train full of munitions had been positioned just next to our own train the entire time. I don't know how she knew this, except that there were probably soldiers on board at some point who tried, unsuccessfully, to remove her and separate her from her trousseau.

At this news, both Diany and Dr. Spencer shuddered. Jimmy perked up and couldn't help but exclaim, "We could have been blown to smithereens!" Dr. Spencer shushed him and said that those kinds of outbursts were likely to upset the other passengers.

As our train slowly left the station, we closed our eyes and tried to get some rest.

I was dozing, recalling Jimmy miming messages to me in the station. I still felt enormous fear and frustration inside, trying to unravel the mystery of his unspoken communication.

"Were you afraid?" I heard a raspy, deep voice ask.

I looked around, my mind still fuzzy and disoriented. We were still on the train. Annie and Jimmy were awake, staring out the windows stoically. Dr. Spencer was sitting in his seat, peering around the edge and down the aisle a bit. I followed his gaze. A gentleman stood with Mrs. Spencer, talking in the raspy, deep voice I recognized from my dream, notebook and pencil in hand. She was animatedly responding in turn.

"What's happening?" I asked, worried that she didn't have her passport.

"That is a reporter, Beverly. He is asking Mrs. Spencer about our night in the train station."

I looked at Dr. Spencer. He had his hand on his brow and his eyes shut. I couldn't hear what Mrs. Spencer was saying, but it seemed she was agitated all over again. The reporter was taking notes, and not quite hiding a sneer.

CHAPTER FOURTEEN – PARIS

We arrived in Paris at 5:00 a.m. instead of 11:00 p.m. the previous day, as we had originally been scheduled. A taxi took us to the Hotel de Crillon where we crawled into bed after some ham sandwiches that Mrs. Spencer had made before we'd left. She kept referring to us as the "little refugees from Belgium." I rather thought we were more world travelers and adventurers, but I was much too sleepy to protest.

In the morning, we had a lovely and plentiful breakfast. Annie was quite excited by the selection and quantity. Later, after a delicious lunch, we went to the Bois de Boulogne, a large public park. The weather was lovely, and we, being rested and well-fed, started to enjoy ourselves at last. Even Diany seemed to have more color and less nerves. That night, we ate Chinese food. It felt like vacation. As we drifted off to sleep, we spoke little, and instead pictured what we might do the next day.

Lying in the comfort of the hotel bed, I dreamt about the President (our car, not the leader of the United States of America). We were inside it and it was so big, even the Spencers were there, and the Jewish family from the Residence Palace, and one of the soldiers who had examined our passports. He was checking our coat pockets for food and stamping our hands when our pockets were empty.

Mrs. Spencer was lying on the floor on top of a trunk of clothes. Her open mouth was like a radio, and military marches were coming out of it. Diany was shivering so hard the car was shaking. But we three kids were throwing paper darts out the window. They flew high into the air and turned into airplanes. The sky was blue and cloudless, and the planes were silver and shaped like birds.

But then the birds began to shriek, or maybe it was Mrs. Spencer's mouth, and someone was shaking me. I felt a hand on my arm, and someone was saying, "Wake up Beverly! Wake up!"

I sat and realized the siren was sounding. We were pulling on our coats and socks and shoes, which we had placed at the ends of our beds just in case this exact thing happened. As we shuffled out into the hall, Annie realized she had on Jimmy's coat, and ran after Jimmy, but he had left with no coat at all, and didn't even have on his shoes and socks.

There were no lights—electricity and gas were always turned off during alerts—but we had a flashlight. When Annie figured out where her coat was, she ran back to the room.

People were running. Diany grabbed my hand and led me towards the stairs. Jimmy was putting his socks and shoes on while going down the stairs. I thought perhaps he might fall, but Jimmy was good on his feet and managed somehow to get both socks and shoes on and barely slow down.

We had agreed ahead of time that should an alert sound, we would meet the Spencers at the bottom of the stairs and go together to the American Embassy shelter. Luckily, they were waiting for us just where we had agreed, and together, we six went out into the black night. It was a little spooky, and even Annie took my hand. I think she was more scared than I was. The air raid siren was the only sound in the heavy silence of the deserted street.

The Embassy had an excellent air raid shelter, and we all stayed there until the "all clear" sounded. We headed back to the hotel and back to sleep until about 7:00 a.m. when another siren went off. Again, we made our way to the Embassy. We looked at magazines to pass the time, then went back to our hotel beds once more when it had ended.

All the next day, we volleyed between lovely vacation-like adventures and air raids. We had a wonderful breakfast and spent the morning in the Tuileries Garden before the first air raid. We had a lunch of sandwiches in Weybert restaurant, rue de la Raise, then spent the afternoon walking along the Champs Élysées.

We had supper in the restaurant Au Cochon de Lait behind the Odéon Theater, and then got a full night's sleep, much needed as we were boarding a train the next day for the coastal town of Arcachon.

In the morning, after another good breakfast, we parted ways with the Spencers. There was a lot of hugging and patting on heads and shoulders from the Spencers, but they also seemed to be in quite a rush to get away, with a lot of, "Well, we must be going" and urgent glances from Mrs. Spencer to her husband.

Daddy had arranged for another friend, Mrs. K. M. Richards, to accompany us from Paris to Arcachon. Her husband had worked with Daddy at some point. She said she'd met us before, but none of us could remember her. We greeted her politely, and shook her soft hand. Her face was heavily powdered and smelled of talc. Her broad top half and her broader bottom half seemed glued together, with the middle part (a waist) nowhere in evidence. Still, she seemed kind and sure of herself, so we put our trust in her and continued on our journey. We left from Gare d'Austerlitz and had an uneventful ride the whole way.

We reached Bordeaux in the afternoon, though we nearly got off at the wrong stop. Just as we were about to get off, Mrs. Richards realized we needed to stay on till the Lateste station. At Lateste, we changed trains and headed for Arcachon, where we took a taxi to Pilat-Plage and the Hotel Haitza. It was nearly dinner time before we finally arrived.

Chapter Fifteen – Hotel Haitza

The Hotel Haitza was on the beach in Arcachon, in the southwest of France. It hid playfully behind a stand of tall pines and faced the Bassin d'Arcachon and the open sea. Though it was only mid-May, the weather was fine and the air smelled like ocean.

The first thing we three kids did after tossing our belongings onto the beds in our room was race each other to the beach, throw off our shoes, and feel the sand and water between our toes. Even Diany smiled and laughed for the first time in many days. The wind off the water felt bracing and fresh. We stayed as long as we could that first day letting the water lap at our legs and running back and forth across the sandy strip between the shore line and the grassy area that led up to the hotel.

That night, I slept soundly and deeply. My dreams were scattered like grains of sand on the wind, snippets of running on the beach and my hair being whipped into my face by a stiff breeze. I woke feeling lazy and quite hungry the next morning.

The hotel was made of white stucco with wide, arched windows and doorways that reminded us all of Rome. Guests could take in a meal or afternoon beverage while enjoying the sea air at the hotel's spectacular outdoor eating area, which backed right up to the sand of the beachfront.

There were many other refugees there (for we were, in fact, refugees at this point), from other areas where the war was encroaching. Among them, a Dutch family from Ghent who owned a factory there, an English woman who befriended Diany, and some new friends for us, Mrs. Portnow and her children.

We also ran into many people we knew already, or who knew Daddy, and so we often took our meals with them. It was a wonderful surprise when our dear friends the Guinns from Antwerp and their son Paul (aka Piggy) arrived a couple days after we did.

Paul's father had been posted in Antwerp. It had taken their family 24 hours to our 12 to reach Paris. They told us their train had actually been machine-gunned. At this, I think we all felt a shiver of excitement, along with a wave of relief that our trip had been less eventful.

We spent those first few days enjoying the beach, getting acclimated, making new friends and reuniting with old ones. Piggy had earned his nickname due to the robust enthusiasm he displayed when presented with a plate of food. He was a good-natured fellow, and happily played the clown at every opportunity.

One night at dinner, Piggy tried to eat his artichoke with a fork and knife. He stuck the fork in, started sawing away at it with his knife, and then, faster than our eyes could perceive, it jumped off his plate and skittered across the floor. We laughed hysterically, and Piggy sat, mouth agape, a comic relief to so much of what we were hearing about the war.

Food was becoming scarce, and we had been looking forward to the Hotel Haitza's menu, as we had been told by many that it was quite good. But we three were less than enthusiastically impressed. It was nothing to rave about, for heaven's sake. Perhaps it was because it wasn't as plentiful or as fresh, but our expectations had been high.

We had fish for nearly every meal, and when we had beef, it was quite tough to chew. I might possibly have stealthily spit mine into my napkin on more than one occasion after an endless bout of chewing had done nothing to disintegrate the meat's stringy fibers.

We didn't require ration cards in France, except for sugar and coal. But there were rules. On Mondays, Tuesdays, and Wednesdays, you could not eat or obtain sweets. On Thursdays, Fridays and Saturdays, there was no meat. We looked forward to Sundays during our five-week stay, because on Sundays, you could have both. One food that quickly became a favorite was *pain au chocolat*. The Guinns had introduced us to this delicious roll with chocolate inside, and we ate it every chance we got.

One day at the end of May, after we had been there about two weeks, Diany came into our rooms quite excited and agitated. She woke us up very early saying, "The directress told us we might have to go away because King Leopold has been a traitor and sacrificed whole armies of French and English soldiers."

Annie, reluctant to wake up, rolled over to try and go back to sleep. Diany kept talking, but finally left us, and we could hear angry, mocking singing in the kitchen just below our room: "*Le roi nous a trahi; il est un lâche*" The king has betrayed us; he is a coward.

It seemed King Leopold had surrendered against the wishes of his advisors, and many felt strongly that this should not have happened. At first I didn't understand why what the King had done had anything to do with us being allowed to stay at the hotel. But things got more and more difficult and precarious for Belgians. In Bordeaux, the large town we were near, it was said that only refugees of Northern France were welcome, and that any Belgians, Dutch, or those from Luxembourg must go to Lot-et-Garonne or other locations. Because Diany was Belgian, it appeared she was no longer welcome.

In the end, the directress decided we need not go. But others started taking the Belgian plates off their cars to avoid trouble, and told us of their shock and surprise at King Leopold's decision.

Diany said, "*Je ne croirai jamais que du Roi Léopold.*" I will never believe that of King Leopold.

Annie became quite angry when other people spoke about it, because no one believed her when she said she didn't blame the king, that he surely had some reason for surrendering. This was not a popular stand to take, however. She got very stern, hands on hips, and her voice would tremble just a little when she became impassioned about something. Politics seemed to be an area that she had many feelings and opinions about.

But most people were either angry with the king, and therefore angry at all Belgians by default, or were scared of being discovered as Belgian and getting some kind of backlash because of the king's decision. Diany spent a lot of time taking us back and forth to the American Embassy in Bordeaux to see Mr. Waterman, the consul there. He was in touch with Mr. Hull, the secretary of state, and both were helping her to get a visa in case we should have to leave for the U.S. Daddy did not wish for us to be separated from Diany, or from each other, which we three kids agreed with wholeheartedly.

It was a confusing time. Sometimes people would tell us we had to leave, then we would see one of Daddy's friends at the Embassy and get permission to stay. Other times we ran out of money, then, just in time, one of Daddy's friends would help us get more. Daddy was trying his very best to care for us from far away, but correspondence and communications of any kind were very difficult.

One day a notice was posted on the hotel door saying that the American steamship *Washington* was leaving on such and such a date and that all who wished to leave must apply for passage before a certain date. We didn't want to go, and Daddy had been very specific that we should NOT go unless necessary, and not to separate. We sought out Mr. Bullitt, the U.S.Ambassador in Paris, who told us that all American citizens must leave the country, especially women and children.

We went to the Embassy to get the appropriate paperwork, but when we got there, we were told Diany could not go with us.

Diany cried, and in her best English said, "We wait for the decision of our father!" meaning, of course, Daddy.

We were all shocked, and held each other tightly. I couldn't imagine travelling without Diany, and it scared us all to think they might force us to. Mr. Waterman looked pale and quite uncomfortable with all of the sudden emotion.

"Well, I can see that this is upsetting to you all," he began as we murmured reassurances to each other and uttered the occasional outraged, but frightened, exclamation.

"I suppose I could write a telegram to Mr. Hull. He is presently with your father, er, Mr. Broy. Perhaps something can be done. But I make no promises!" he quickly added.

And then, right then and there, he wrote out a message to be telegrammed to Mr. Hull that pleaded our case, saying none of wished to be separated, and that it was Daddy's wish that we not be.

We left Mr. Waterman's office only slightly mollified. We continued to stay in close physical proximity, arms around one another. We took the train back to Pilat Plage feeling none too good and worried about the outcome. When we arrived, things were only worse.

It seemed many of our friends were planning on leaving, including the Guinns, and also the Conkwrights and the Portnow family. Even Mr. Portnow, who had bronchitis bordering on pneumonia, was going to leave, against the advice of his doctor. All were taking the ship back to the United States. It is a hard thing to stay put when most are going off in one direction.

"It will be all right," Diany kept repeating, as much, I think, to herself as to us. "Mr. Waterman will get the telegram to Mr. Hull. Your father will not allow anyone to separate us."

Over the next week or so, we began to watch our friends settling up bills in preparation for checking out, with hurried movements, as though an encroaching lava flow were imminent. One day while assembled in the lobby, one of our friends, Mrs. Cross, approached. She was in Arcachon alone, while her husband remained at his diplomatic post.

Mrs. Cross looked around to be sure no one was listening, then leaned in towards us, speaking in hushed tones. We all leaned in too, to hear her.

"This is strictly confidential. I am only sharing it with you because I think you will understand my motives. It is my intention to NOT take the ship back to America. Instead, I will be traveling by car to Portugal."

We all looked at each other, questions on our faces. Diany seemed puzzled, as though she hadn't heard correctly.

"But, of course you must take the ship, my friend," Diany said, part statement and part question. "All the Americans are being ordered to leave on it, yes?"

"Strictly speaking," Mrs. Cross continued, "that is true. But just between you and me, it is my opinion that moving further south will prove to be a safer alternative. Yes, the Germans have invaded Paris. But this is certainly no cause for concern. Portugal is far enough away that it shall be quite safe. Frankly, I'm not so sure about traveling by ship!"

I shuddered a little, remembering Jimmy's conversation with Mummy about ocean mines and German subs.

"I have enough room in my car for the four of you," Mrs. Cross continued. "What I'm suggesting, Diany dear, is that you and the children come with me to Portugal."

We all felt quite stunned. On the one hand, this was a shocking idea, ignoring the government's edict about leaving. On the other hand, it quite solved the problem of whether Diany would be permitted to come with us or not.

"I thank you sincerely, Mrs. Cross," Diany began. "We must wait to hear what the Embassy says and follow the wishes of our father, Mr. Broy."

"Yes, yes, dear," Mrs. Cross clucked. "Of course. But the offer stands firm. I will be leaving within the week, and I would love the company on the drive."

With that, Mrs. Cross made her polite excuses and left. Diany shepherded us back to our rooms where we could speak more privately.

As soon as we shut the door behind us, we all started talking at once.

"Children, children!" Diany said. "We cannot hear one another if we all shout at the same time. Anne, you are the oldest. What do you think of this?"

"Well," Annie began. She looked suddenly hesitant to share her thoughts, though only moments before she had been angling to be heard above the rest of us. "I—I agree with Mrs. Cross that further south is better. But I don't know if we should break the rules." Annie was a very strict rule follower in most instances, ledge-walking notwithstanding.

"Jimmy, what is it you wanted to say?" Diany asked. He had been biting his lip and gripping hem of his shirt, waiting for his turn.

"I think it's a grand idea! The open sea is not safe! And we don't even know if you can come with us, Diany. And who shall be waiting on the other side?" I had never heard Jimmy show fear and uncertainty, but I detected a hint of both in his voice now.

"I see. And Beverly, what about you?"

I felt suddenly shy as all their eyes turned toward me. I wasn't used to having much of a say in decisions, and this felt like an important one.

"Well, I...I am not fond of long drives. And we don't speak Portuguese. But I'm game for it if it allows us to stay with you, Diany."

"That's right Sis!" Jimmy exclaimed, happy I was all in.

"Well, I see that you are all in agreement about this," Diany began. "However, the truth is, we must wait and see. We cannot make this decision on our own. We must hear from our father and from the Embassy."

It was hard to sleep that night, not knowing, yet again, what our future held. I dreamt I was on a ship. It was stormy, and the wind was fierce. Waves kept washing over the side of the ship, dousing us all and nearly knocking us down. I looked to my left. Jimmy was there, holding a sword out as if about to charge upon the sea. To my right was Annie, keeping a list in a notebook. I could see the words she was writing, even though it was dark. At the top of the page, she had written, "Rules We Are Breaking" and then a numbered list. I couldn't see them all, but the first was, "Ignoring the U.S. Government."

I suddenly realized Diany was nowhere to be seen, and I began running up and down the deck, calling her name.

It was then I saw a figure standing on the deck before me. It was a woman, but I couldn't make out her features—she was all in shadow. Her hands were on her hips. "Come here, Beverly," she seemed to be saying, though her voice was lost on the wind. I walked towards her, all the while being pushed about the deck like a Bagatelle ball.

"Diany?" I called. The woman stood still. I walked closer and could see she was wearing a fine hat on top of her head. I squinted to see her better as the storm raged around me, filling my ears with the sound of waves and roaring gales.

My toe hit something hard, and I looked down. A large metallic circle with letters on it stood in my path. "M-I-N-E." I leapt back in surprise, then jumped over it. Suddenly dozens more appeared on the deck, and I had to hop and jump and zig-zag to avoid them, all the while not getting any closer to the woman ahead of me.

Though the storm whipped all around me, the woman's coat, her hat, and her hair all remained in place, perfectly arranged. Just as I stepped over what appeared to be the last mine, nearly close enough to recognize the woman, a spray of cold sea water splashed in my face.

"Beverly!" I heard Annie shout. "Beverly, shut the window!"

Seeing as I was outside, I didn't grasp how I could shut a window.

"Beverly!" I felt a shove from my right. Then another spray of water. I opened my eyes and realized I was not, in fact, on a ship at all. I was in my bed by the open window. A rainstorm had blown in from the sea and was showering me, and Annie beside me. I sat up, scooted closer to the window, damp sheets and blankets in my path, and shut the window. Water lay in a pool on the sash, and the sleeve of my nightdress soaked it up like a sponge. I was too tired to get up and change, so I moved as far from the window as I could, tried to find a dry patch to lie in, and fitfully fell back into slumber.

* * * * *

It was only a few days later that we heard back from Mr. Waterman at the Embassy. He was getting Diany's papers in order, and was then able to give her permission to leave with us to the U.S. Another friend, Dr. Labat, gave her a medical certificate. Diany was able to get copies of her birth certificate and an exit visa, so it seemed that we would be going on the ship together.

This was a huge relief, but we were not sure what this meant as far as seeing Daddy again. Who would meet us in the States? Did Mummy know we were coming back? Was Daddy coming too, or did he have to stay in Brussels? What would life there be like? For though Annie and Jimmy had been there, they didn't remember it at all, and I had never been. We didn't know the answers to any of these questions, but we at least no longer had to fear separating from Diany.

We told Mrs. Cross we would be taking the ship, and though she seemed disappointed, she wished us well and patted our arms with a pitying smile on her face.

We slowly began gathering our belongings and drying out any wet garments in preparation for our departure. As I pulled down my swimming suit from the window, I looked towards the sea. From here, it seemed inviting, a source of the happiness and fun times we'd all shared at the Hotel Haitza.

We'd spent the past five weeks splashing in the water and taking meals in the eating area beneath the pines. I was sad to be leaving, and just a little nervous about our voyage. It was no small consolation that Diany would remain with us, no matter what the next leg of our journey brought. But I was just a tiny bit scared of going on the ship, of feeling seasick or falling overboard, but mostly of mines and leaving Daddy.

I wondered too what life in America would be like. I had never been there, though of course knew a lot about it from Bonnie and Aunt Anna and Uncle John, as well as Aunt Bernice. And we knew Mummy and her family would be there. But it was rather like trying to put back on a dress you'd worn two seasons ago. It didn't quite fit, and the styles had changed, so it felt awkward and restrictive.

Annie and Jimmy had been working on being mature and refined. I don't know if it was for my benefit, or for Mummy's, but they were saying overly optimistic statements all the time like, "We shall get to experience all sorts of new adventures once we're in America!" or, "We shall certainly seem exotic to the children there, what with knowing more than one language!"

I didn't know how I felt about any of that, but I did have a secret desire to shop at an American department store.

Only a day or two before we were to leave, while Diany was finishing up the last of her paperwork, we received word from Mr. Waterman. He had heard from Paris, and Daddy had said in no uncertain terms that he did NOT want us to go on that ship. It seemed he had some of the same fears about how we would find one another again should we leave for U.S. soil.

His decision was a surprise and caused a rather abrupt change in plans. It was also a bit of a predicament, as with every day that passed, watching others depart, we felt the war coming closer. It truly no longer felt safe to stay.

In the end, Mr. Waterman was able to contact Mr. Cross at his post, and the decision to accompany Mrs. Cross to Portugal was finalized. She was both happy and relieved to have our company. We packed our bags once more, and left for Lisbon.

CHAPTER SIXTEEN – MONTE ESTORIL

We spent the first night of our journey with Mrs. Cross at the large Hotel Maria Cristina in San Sebastian, Spain, where the Urumea River flows to the sea, just twelve miles from the French border. It was our job to help navigate, using maps Mrs. Cross had procured and measuring as best we could the distance using the map key's kilometer equivalents. It was just over 230 kilometers from Arcachon to San Sebastian.

The next day we travelled another 200 plus kilometers and had lunch in Burgos. Then it was on through Salamanque, approximately 240 kilometers further. Jimmy showed us how to use our thumb nails to approximate one centimeter, converting every centimeter to 10 kilometers, as the map legend dictated. Doing the measuring and math kept us busy on our long drive, and we took turns verifying each other's calculations.

Mrs. Cross' car was a Chrysler New Yorker. She'd had it shipped from the US, and told us it was the only car she felt comfortable driving. I found the seats hard and rigid, while Jimmy found its mechanical and design features inferior to Daddy's car. He attempted to engage Mrs. Cross in comparisons between her car and Daddy's (superior) President, but she waved away his comments, claiming not to have the interest nor the inclination with which to discuss cars.

Gasoline was hard to come by, and Mrs. Cross hadn't much Spanish money left. When she paid for gas in Salamanque, she had to convince the man to take her French cash. We filled several gas cans as well as the tank of the car, because gas stations were few and far between. As the trunk was full of our luggage, the gas cans sat on the floor between our collective legs and feet. The pungent liquid sloshed and lapped against the sides of the metal cans, the smell filling the car. We rolled down the windows and let the warm air from the surrounding countryside cool our skin and help flush out the fumes.

Once we passed through Salamanque, Mrs. Cross stayed as close to the border of Spain and Portugal as possible, looking for the best route over the border. Spain was struggling through its own civil war at the time, and she felt it would be best if we didn't linger there. We hoped to cross the border before night, as the roads were quite bad.

"They don't appear to want to encourage friendship with Portugal!" Mrs. Cross joked, implying the road conditions were an intentional barrier.

We had just passed a small village and were about to go up a hill, but the setting sun was directly in Mrs. Cross' eyes, so she stopped to put more gas in the tank while we waited for it to set. Jimmy helped her haul out one of the gas cans and a tin funnel. He held the funnel while she poured the gas carefully through it into the tank. Jimmy had gotten quite good at sensing when enough had been poured, watching for the funnel to back up just a little as she poured slowly.

Before long, the orange ball of the sun dropped into a melted puddle of itself just visible above the horizon. Mrs. Cross climbed back behind the steering wheel, not wanting to waste another moment. As she turned the key in the ignition, however, nothing happened. She tried again, but still nothing, not even that dreary sound cars sometimes make when they want to start but just can't seem to get the gumption up to do it.

"Well this is rather unfortunate," she muttered, getting back out of the car. Some peasants from the nearby village were walking past, on their way towards home, we assumed. They began pointing at us, seemingly quite astonished to see a woman driving a car with only another woman and some children for company.

Then they approached the car. They spoke in fast and animated Spanish, and they seemed quite friendly, as if they wanted to help.

As none of us spoke much Spanish, we instead began handing out chocolate and sugar. War had taken a toll on Spain, and the people were excited and happy about our gifts. Soon, the entire village came out, even the priest and little babies. One man kept gesturing and speaking intently to Mrs. Cross.

"What does he want?" Jimmy asked, fascinated by the people and their curious ways.

"I think he's saying he knows where to get help," answered Mrs. Cross. "As we have no choice, we shall just have to wait here." Then she turned to the man and said, "Sí, señor," nodding her head and smiling.

The man walked hurriedly off down the road, and we got comfortable, stretching our legs and sitting on the ground with some of the local children who were simultaneously shy and curious.

We all sort of stared at one another, and once in a while one of the younger children would come to touch our hair and faces, then run back to their mothers.

After a long while, the man returned with another man. The new man was smiling and seemed happy to help, though he looked quite tired. He asked Mrs. Cross for a pump, which they somehow communicated to one another with hand signals and gestures.

Once she figured out what he was saying, she shook her head "no," telling him she hadn't got one. He wandered away again, muttering. He didn't look angry so much as weary. We waited some more while the village children played around us and the babies nursed, cried, and napped. The sun had finished its descent, and though it had gotten darker, we could still see.

Diany was leaning against a tree, and a little girl, maybe two years old, approached her. She stood before Diany, who, though surprised, smiled back at the toddler's intent but trusting face. Then, the little girl placed her hand on Diany's cheek and stood staring at her. Diany gently placed her hand on top of the girl's and smiled back. It was hard to see in the waning light, but it almost looked as if Diany were about to cry. I wondered if she was sad that the little girl was poor and hungry, or possibly Diany was simply exhausted and easily emotional. Annie got that way sometimes when she was frustrated or confused. I didn't see the point of it. Why cry? It solved nothing and usually left you with a blotchy face and puffy eyes.

Eventually the man returned with a hose. His friend, the man who had brought him, held a lantern over the open hood. After blowing several times through the pipes and tubes using the hose he'd procured, he managed to start the car. It seemed something had been clogging one of the tubes, and he had blown long enough and hard enough to dislodge it. I didn't ask where the clog had moved to.

By now it was fully dark. The babies and smaller children had fallen asleep, curled up in their mothers' laps, thumbs in their mouths. We thanked the people many times, saying, "*Gracias*" and smiling and waving as we climbed back into the car.

Mrs. Cross gave the mechanic some American cash, explaining in her broken Spanish that she had no more Spanish money. "*No más dinero, no más,*" she kept repeating when he gazed at the American bills with a puzzled look on his face.

He finally accepted the money, looking unsure. As we pulled off, everybody said in chorus, "*Adiós!*" We answered, "*Adiós!*" and vowed to come back and visit them all on our way back through, though none of us could have predicted when that might be.

The remainder of our drive that night felt unusually long and bumpy. We were weary of the road and the interior of Mrs. Cross' car, though grateful for her hospitality and chauffeur services. We could no longer read the map, and the space in the back seat felt cramped. Jimmy kept shoving me saying, "Stay on your part of the seat. I can barely fit." Then I, who sat in the middle between Jimmy and Annie, would inch as much as I could away from Jimmy, but that much closer to Annie, who would complain, "Bev, I'm too hot for you to be touching me," in a somewhat irritated voice.

When we finally reached the border, after miles of twisting, narrow mountain roads, the guards told us the border was closed for the night. No amount of persuading would change their minds.

Mrs. Cross inquired about lodging, and we picked our way down a dark road and found an inn for the night. We got two rooms, one with a double bed for Jimmy and me, and a single bed for Diany, and the other with a single bed that Mrs. Cross and Annie had to share. As we drifted off to sleep in our rather primitive accommodations, we were serenaded outside the windows by someone singing a lovely Spanish lullaby.

My dreams had no pictures that night, only sounds. I heard the crying of the babies outside the village we had broken down near; I heard the sound of the car engine starting and stalling; I heard the crunching of gravel under tires and the rapid-fire speech of the border guards; I heard the sweet tones of a Spanish lullaby and faint snoring from Diany; I heard my own heart beating and the blood rushing through my veins; I heard a tiny voice inside my head, or perhaps an echo saying, "Fly to safety, little bird."

But it was the sound of Jimmy's feet hitting the floor in the morning that woke me. I think I had been waiting all night for a sign that it was time to leave. I had gotten rather used to leaving. It hadn't gotten any more comfortable, but it was at least familiar. I woke with no problem and no prodding, ready to head out again. I didn't much relish the idea of returning to Mrs. C's car, but a strong desire to finally arrive at our destination had taken over all of us. For me, I was prepared for gas fumes and cramped, stiff seating if it meant finally ending our journey.

Mrs. Cross had found a bedbug in the bed she and Annie shared, so she decided we should move on immediately, not even eating first. She seemed as anxious to get to Lisbon as we were, and hustled us to the car as soon as we were toileted and dressed.

After we crossed the border, we found some breakfast in a small cafe. However, the number of flies made eating extremely difficult. Every time we would shoo them away, three more would arrive, resting on our food or buzzing in our faces.

We were hungry and managed to drink our *café con leche* and eat our croissants despite the pesky flies. After breakfast, Annie and I found a doll in a Portuguese costume at a small outdoor market. Mrs. Cross bought it for us, for which we were extremely appreciative. I think she felt sorry for us with all this driving and homelessness.

Driving through Coimbra, where the flies were even worse, we stopped for lunch. We encountered many donkeys on the road and lots of people coming back from the market carrying jugs and baskets on their heads. It made for slow travel, but vivid memories.

It was evening when we finally reached Lisbon. We searched for a hotel, but they were all full. Many refugees had been coming to Lisbon, as more and more countries had been invaded.

I suddenly remembered how at Christmastime, Mummy would tell us the story of the Virgin Mary and Joseph knocking on doors, trying to find a place to sleep, when all the inns were full. They ended up in a manger. I wondered if that would be our fate as well.

In the end, we drove west of Lisbon to Estoril, where there was a resort on the coast. By the time we arrived at the Grand Hotel Italia, we three kids had fallen asleep, our heads at odd angles to our shoulders, resulting in stiff cricks. There, we feasted on a supper of cold meat and chicken, bread and butter, and fruit. It was one of the best meals I could remember having in a long time, and particularly delicious because there was no onslaught of flies or imminent threat of having to return to the car.

After dinner, we immediately retired to our rooms. No one objected or tried to draw out good nights. Diany and Annie slept next door to Jimmy and I, and Mrs. Cross was in a third room, all of us opposite the bathroom.

As I lay my head on the pillow, I turned to Jimmy. His eyes were still half open, though his breathing had slowed to a steady rhythm.

"Broy?" I half whispered.

"Hmm?" he responded, barely aware he'd made a sound.

"Are you having fun?"

His brow furrowed a little in the dim light.

"I mean," I continued tentatively, "this is a grand adventure, isn't it?"

"Yes, grand adventure," he mumbled. Then he turned his back to me, and promptly fell into the sleep of the dead, his shoulders sinking even further into the pillows and mattress.

I knew I wasn't far behind in falling asleep, but one last thought played at the edges of my awareness. The last 48 hours or so hadn't been as much fun as one would hope to have on a grand adventure, but as long as it was still an adventure, I could expect it to feel fun again soon. I decided to believe Jimmy, and drifted into my dreams.

*   *   *   *   *

I stood at the intersection of two roads. Signs pointed in each direction, labeled with destinations. One said, "America." Another said, "Residence Palace." A third said, "Germans, This Way!" And the fourth read, "Lowther Road."

At each corner of the intersection were cafés, and people eating outdoors. Flies buzzed around them, but there seemed to be an invisible field around me that no flies could cross.

I was eating a particularly sticky orange. Juice was dripping all over my hands and chin, onto my blouse. I let it dribble out of my mouth, teasing the flies as they buzzed outside my bubble.

No cars came down either of the roads. I wiped my hands on my skirt and focused my attention on what was around me. When I did this, everything miraculously magnified and I could see exactly what each person was eating. One boy was trying to take a bite of his croissant, but every time it got close to his mouth, it would become encased in flies and he would cry to his mother, who only waved toward him in a shushing motion.

I found I could hear the people, too. The mother was talking to an important man and the man was saying something to her about appointments and votes. She was nodding and asked for "clarification." Then, oddly, she seemed to know I was listening, and she turned to look at me. When she turned, I saw she had Mummy's eyes.

I awoke to the sound of the sea, and a breakfast of toast, butter, honey, marmalade, and coffee. By the time we finished eating, I had forgotten my dream and felt the call of the sea. The entire day, Jimmy, Annie, Diany, and I played at the beach, enjoying the sunshine and surf and the mild temperatures.

Monte Estoril was by far the most relaxing and fun place we had stayed yet. We spent every day at the beach from then on, getting sunburned. In the beginning, we would change our clothes behind the rocks, until we realized a group of boys was watching us from their perch on a wall some distance away. That ended that.

After we played on the beach all day, we would return to large plates of fresh fruit. We made many new friends. The children and parents we met all seemed to feel sorry for us because we were on our adventure without Daddy. We often shared meals, drawing our tables together.

Sometimes I would listen to the half-whispered discussion between the adults. They always talked about the war, about the Germans, about which cities had "fallen" or were "occupied." Jimmy and Annie would sometimes try and join the conversation, but Diany and the other grown ups seemed to want to keep the details to themselves. We all wanted to know what was going on, but at the same time we didn't want to break the spell of the vacation-like quality of our stay. It reminded me of being at a party, and even though you're tired and the music has stopped, you want one more game, one more dance, one more cupcake.

My newest friend was named Serge. He was older than me by a few years, and had lovely golden hair. I sometimes got lost in observing the sun's reflection off of it. Serge's father was a writer, and Serge had several brothers and sisters who we all enjoyed spending time with.

When I was with Serge, he always smiled at me like he could see my thoughts. This usually left me feeling a little fluttery inside, as though a small bird was trying to escape from my heart.

One night while I was visiting his room, Serge climbed onto his bed and sat beneath the covers, snug and cozy.

"Beverly, come up here with me," he said, inviting me to get snuggly and cozy too. I giggled and ran away, my heart pitter-pattering the whole time. By the time I got back to my room, my breath was coming in short bursts and my heart was hammering.

If we weren't spending the day at the beach, we were exploring the town's many gardens with their exotic flowers. There was an ancient manor, Cintra, that stood straight above the mountain and had been the home of Portuguese queens. To reach it, we had to drive up some very steep and dangerous roads.

One garden in town belonged to a rich Englishman who was mad for flowers and other beautiful plants. We strolled through the gardens, admiring the colors and variety. I had a pang of remembrance for Huck's roses back on Lowther Road, and found myself urgently missing him. This feeling made me squirmy and itchy, so I focused on some unusual plants with large leaves and no flowers whatsoever.

One day we visited Praia das Maçãs, or Beach of Apples. It was the Westernmost part of Europe and there were different explanations of how it got its odd name. A local woman told us that long ago, apples would fall off the trees upstream of the river that flows along the southern side of the beach. The apples would then wash up on the beach.

But a hotel waiter had a different explanation, saying it was because a large boat transporting fruit had shipwrecked many, many years ago. The fruit floated ashore, and thus the name. Either way, we imagined what people must have thought when they woke to find apples all over the sand. Perhaps they thought, "Breakfast!"

That night in my dreams, I was floating and bobbing in the waves, and all around me were not only apples, but all manner of delicious fruit—mangoes and bananas and guava and fresh figs, all bobbing within reach. I could smell them and I woke the next morning ravenous and craving fresh fruit as though I'd perish without it. Fortunately, there was plenty available and I gorged myself on all of it, whether crispy apples or fleshy mangoes. I savored every juicy bite, the flavors dancing on my tongue.

After we had spent about three weeks in Monte Estoril, we finally heard from Daddy. Within the course of two days, we received a letter and got two phone calls from him, one while he was in San Sebastian, and the other from Madrid. He said he missed us and was working very hard to get to us as quickly as he could, slowly making his way south in the President. He said he couldn't bear to be away from us any longer, and that he felt it was actually safer if we were together than so far from him where it was so difficult to send money and get messages through.

In the end, Daddy got help from a man named Mr. Miller, who notified us we would be meeting Daddy in Madrid and helped arrange for our departure. There were exit visas and things he had to do and take care of in Lisbon, but all of us were very excited at the prospect of being with Daddy again.

As we prepared for our reunion, a reporter named Mr. Treanor from the *L.A. Times* in the United States came to call. He was stationed in Europe looking for human interest stories, and had heard about the three American children and their governess. He interviewed all of us kids, asking about our travels and what we thought of this war. He actually suggested I might have cried in fear during the air raids! I didn't dignify that question with an answer.

CHAPTER SEVENTEEN – REUNITED

We departed at 4:00 a.m. for Cintra Airfield on July 9th, 1940. It was dark and the air was cool when we stumbled out of our sleep and into the pre-dawn morning. One of our few remaining friends drove us the 13.4 kilometers in eerie silence before most were awake.

Diany, however, was wide awake and nervous as a bird, fluttering from one to the other of us to make sure we'd remembered all our belongings and used the bathroom before leaving our rooms. She had packed us bread and fruit from dinner the night before, where we'd shared a table one last time with our dwindling circle of friends, many of whom were preparing to leave on the next steamer back to the U.S.

Even Mrs. Cross, our stalwart companion on the road from Arcachon to Monte Estoril, had finally relented and agreed to exit the continent. At our final dinner together, she sheepishly admitted that her husband's support of her independent streak had dwindled as the situation with the Germans and the war had become increasingly serious and continued to move closer to us, no matter where we seemed to scatter.

"I don't suppose I can continue to worry him so," she mumbled, somehow embarrassed by the admission. "He cares for me so, and I see the wisdom in leaving now." Then, in one last fiery breath, "But those damnable Germans shall NOT prevail!"

There were hugs all around as the few of us who were left prepared for our final departures. Some cried, but we were too excited about seeing Daddy to feel sad. We all wished one another well and even thanked the wait staff profusely for all their kind attentiveness during our stay.

At the airfield, we went through customs and presented our passports to the guards. It seemed to go on forever. We were all sleepy but extremely worked up about seeing Daddy again.

Finally, we were allowed to board our plane and take off for Madrid. The sound of the propellers could easily have drowned out our ever-more-alert enthusiastic exclamations, but we were committed to our bubbly chatter by this point.

As our plane touched down, we all had our faces pressed to the glass to see if we could see Daddy. Diany clapped like a little girl when we finally came to a stop, her smile as wide as her face, seemingly just as impatient to be reunited as we were.

We ran down the portable staircase into Daddy's arms. There was a lot of hugging and kissing and jumping up and down. He took each of our faces, even Diany's, and looked right into our eyes and said he missed us so.

He had tears in his eyes as he stood back and took in the fact that we were all together again. He thanked Diany with deep looks into her eyes and his hands pressed firmly over hers. Her eyes were brimming with tears as she smiled and nodded, trembling ever so slightly.

From there, we drove to the Palace Hotel in Madrid in the President, our long-lost friend. After so much bumping about in Mrs. Cross's car, the smooth-riding President was a welcome luxury. We dined outside on the hotel patio, but I was far too excited to eat all my food.

We chatted and caught up, each sharing a different part of our adventures over the last two months. I suddenly felt, more than saw, movement behind me. The next thing I knew, an arm and hand reached over my shoulder and grabbed the scraps from my plate. In that short, blurred moment, I noted the arm was skinny and the hand dirty. I was too surprised to react; everyone else just stared for a moment, still as statues.

Then Daddy explained. "My dears, I know that was shocking to you. But do try and understand...the Spanish people are starving, and someone far hungrier than Dearsie has taken what he needed to survive."

I didn't feel angry or scared, just a little sad for the people. I almost wished I'd eaten less than I had.

In my dreams that night, I felt a hunger, and looked around me to a ring of bushes, trees and rocks. Though I couldn't see them, I somehow knew that behind each tree trunk and crouching behind each boulder and shivering in each shrub were Spaniards, hungrily watching and waiting.

I felt in my pockets but found only crumbs. I threw them and they landed in the grass and dirt. Hundreds of black birds flew out of every branch and descended on the crumbs without a sound.

Over the next few days, we stayed at different points along the route back to Brussels. We stayed in Burgos, where we met a young American we had known in Bordeaux. We passed through Biaritz in the Pyrenees. Next came a small town where we stayed in a hotel run by a woman who was a Belgian refugee.

The feeling of adventure had been replaced with a gentle longing for home. The driving and the stops that punctuated it were a means to an end marking off each city and border crossing.

Once in France, we visited the consulate in Bordeaux, where we had dinner and were given coupons for gasoline. This was the only way to get gas anymore, and the coupons were more precious than gold.

At dinner, Daddy talked business with his colleagues but was unusually attentive to each of us, smiling and touching our shoulders and including us in the conversation. We noticed the difference and accepted it as our new normal, now that we all felt a deep appreciation for one another. After so much separation by miles, governments, and warring parents, just to be together was a precious gift.

On the way to Poitiers, we stopped in a small town where the German military had taken over the hotel. A charming officer took care of us and would not accept payment for procuring our rooms. His English was perfect! And his boots were polished to such a high gleam that I could scarcely take my eyes off them. Americans were still treated respectfully by the Germans as we were not (yet) at war with one another. It was hard to believe all the stories we'd heard of their cruelty when we were treated so kindly by the soldiers we encountered.

We found gasoline the next day, bolstered by more coupons from the mayor of the town. All along the road were enormous trucks in caravans. There were abandoned corpses of cars along the way as well, damaged or out of gas. Some tanks and cars were marked "Postal Service." Had the mail stopped being delivered while we were gone?

In Poitiers, we stayed at a boarding house along with many other travelers. The service was limited and we had to serve ourselves. There was a long wooden table, slightly scarred and stained with water marks. On it stood a sugar bowl, a butter dish, and a plate of sliced bread. That was all. I don't think any of us cared much. We spread our bread with butter, sprinkled it with sugar, and felt nourished by the feeling of being a family again.

Then we headed for Tours. The surrounding countryside had been bombed quite extensively and we saw many ruins. It was impossible to find any place to eat, as all the restaurants had been requisitioned by the German army. At last, we found a little inn that miraculously had plenty of food which we wolfed down ravenously.

Along the road that evening, we picnicked on food we'd brought from the inn. We could go no further in the dark, as we could no longer see the road. Just as we were figuring out sleeping arrangements in the President, with Daddy taking a watch while we slept, some people holding lights appeared and invited to stay in a refugee camp.

We followed the Frenchman who had found us about a half mile down a scruffy path. We three kids (even Jimmy!) were given beds in the women's section, along with Diany, but Daddy went back to sleep in the President. I think he was worried it might not be there in the morning if he left it alone. We hated being apart, and I felt bad for Daddy, wondering if even the President's large back seat was long enough for Daddy to sleep on.

That night, as people all around me snored, I pushed my body as close to Diany's as possible. We shared a bunk, not because I needed someone watching over me or out of fear, but because beds were limited.

Annie slept next to another girl. I could tell she was unhappy about it, and a little nervous by the way her face went still upon hearing the news. But from what we could tell, the other people were just as tired as we were, and there really was no energy for discomfort.

The next morning, we wasted no time leaving. The bathroom was dirty and uncomfortable, and I had to hold my nose when using it, being careful where to step. Diany kept us close, and we suffered through the trials of maneuvering through bunks of people while being stiff from our lumpy cots, and rumpled after sleeping in our clothes. But we made the best of it, and found Daddy waiting for us outside the shelter. We left, happy to be on our way.

Soon after we left, the President ran out of gas, and we began to roll as far as we could on our way to Paris. After a time, we came to rest on a flat and rutted, road, unable to roll any farther. Some Belgian officers from a Red Cross post nearby were able to give us some gas. It wasn't much, but it was enough to resume our journey.

We found no places to eat, everything abandoned or empty. We continued for miles and miles, rolling when possible to save on gas, without finding anything. At one stop, the owner of a restaurant gave us a table and chairs, but had no food to offer.

Near Paris, the road to the capital was blocked. So we detoured to Versailles, just outside the city limits. Once there, we were able to buy some food to satisfy our hunger. We rolled on and on without stopping until we found lodging.

It was in Mons, Belgium at the border of France that we found a small inn with food enough to seem like a feast; soup, chicken, salad, apple compote, coffee and wine.

Though relieved and thankful, all around us were reminders that battles had been fought and war had raged right where we were. Everywhere we saw ruins and entire farms destroyed, looking like ghostly skeletons or shells.

It was after 5:00 p.m., almost 12 hours after we had set out from the refugee camp, when we finally reached Brussels and the Residence Palace on rue de la Loi. Things had changed greatly since we were last there.

CHAPTER EIGHTEEN – HOME

A German soldier stood guard, blocking our entrance to the Residence Palace. He stood erect, his boots polished and his leather belt tight around his waist. Though he was congenial enough, smiling slightly and showing no hostility towards us, still, he told us we were not permitted to come in.

"Nein, Sie sind nicht berechtigt, ohne entsprechende Papiere geben. Ich entschuldige mich, aber ich kann nicht zulassen, dass Sie weitergeben." No, you are not allowed to enter without appropriate papers. I apologize, but I can not let you pass.

Daddy was quite put out about this and began to argue with the guard. We realized Daddy was tired, but it frightened us to see him start an altercation with an armed soldier, though the young German maintained a calm, steadfast stance while refusing to let us cross the threshold.

Diany miraculously produced from within her bags a pass from the Air Force Commander of Belgium/Northern France that gave permission to enter the building. The Germans are nothing if not sticklers for rules and the appropriate paperwork. He had to let us in after that.

Upon entering, we found the entire building had been requisitioned by the German Air Ministry, and nearly all the beautiful apartments had been made into offices. Typewriters clacked away, and dozens of uniformed Nazi soldiers busily and briskly walked the halls or sat at desks.

Against all odds, our apartment on the top floor had remained untouched. Daddy and Diany seemed quite concerned about the changes that had taken place in our absence. Still, that very evening, a musical corps gave a recital for the officers and their staffs, and invited us to join them. The Germans were quite polite and civil, and though we were tired from our journey, we accepted the hospitality and enjoyed the comforts of being back to our familiar, if much-changed, home.

That first night back, I dreamt of soldiers. They were faceless, or all had the same face, but without expression. They were everywhere, at every corner, in every room and hallway, on the stairs, even in the bathroom. Some of them ignored me, but others said, "*Nein, du kannst nicht eintreten,*" blocking my way, but never looking at me. Sometimes I would tug on their sleeve, but they never budged.

An uncomfortable feeling of being unwelcome in our own home persisted throughout the following days. We didn't suffer that feeling for long.

Just days after we arrived, the Germans installed an anti-aircraft gun directly above our apartment roof. It became impossible to sleep with all the noise. Sleep-deprived and grouchy, Daddy concluded we should move out. We temporarily stayed at the Miller Boarding House while Daddy began a search for a more suitable residence.

Our new routine became to wake at the boarding house, eat some breakfast, then head over to the Residence Palace, where we would spend hours packing up all the odds and ends we planned to take. At lunch and in the evening, we'd return to the boarding house, giving ourselves short breaks from the arduous task.

The Germans accommodated our back and forthing. It didn't seem like they wanted us there, but at the same time, recognized we were making a move out of the building, which was the end result they desired. As we'd enter and exit several times a day, the guard would dutifully let us pass. But a new stiffness became detectable beneath his emotionless veneer. The officers we'd encounter in the entryway and halls gave clipped nods with pursed lips, always curt, never rude. And yet, with each day, there grew a discomfort and uneasiness, along with a feeling of being shut out with barely a drop of patience to spare.

Luckily, Daddy found us a new home at the former residence of the Ambassador, John Cudahy. He had been recalled to America right around the time we were in Portugal, and his home in the Palais d'Assche was now available. As both the Residence Palace and Palais d'Assche were fully furnished, we only packed personal belongings.

It had a solid look about it, rather box-like, but regal nonetheless. A glorious arch encased with a rainbow of bricks marked the entrance. The building appeared deceptively small from the outside, disguising its grand scale and history of opulence.

Inside was quite another story. The Palais had ninety-eight rooms, and was the former residence of a count and a marquesse. This gave our new home a sense of nobility. The walls held plaques commemorating the birth of none other than King Leopold himself. But the Palais d'Assche no longer housed royalty; only American ambassadors, and now a consul.

We had a garden, as well as a garage, and a big Stars and Stripes flew outside the upstairs balcony. We occupied the third floor, made up of six bedrooms, three bathrooms, a dining room, living room, and pantry.

On the fourth floor, originally used to house domestic help, we stored all our furniture, as the residence was already furnished. The kitchen and laundry were in the basement. We kids enjoyed our freedom to roam and relished the return to all the creature comforts we'd done without during our travels.

During our explorations of the palace, we found hidden rooms and secret doorways, which led to hours of hide and seek games. We also rather fell in love with the dumbwaiter that could be used to transport our meals up from the kitchen to the dining room. Jimmy wasted no time testing it to see if it could also transport boys of a certain age.

The library was so much bigger and better stocked than Daddy's library had been at the Residence Palace. We had at our fingertips books on practically every subject, and many in different languages as well.

We missed our spacious apartment high above Brussels, but our new space was certainly an adventure in and of itself. With large pillars to climb and trenches to investigate, we found plenty to keep us busy and entertained.

During our stay at Palais d'Assche, Diany learned to ride a bike and took rides to the forest and along the streets. She seemed happier and more relaxed than we'd seen her in months. We'd all go for outings to the local newspaper and candy store, where we'd buy Black Jack chewing gum with its sharp licorice flavor.

The other thing we discovered was that many Belgians appreciated an American presence. On many occasions, we would find notes on our door saying things like, *"Vous êtes nos amis."* Our American flag hanging outside the balcony was a beacon that attracted those seeking friendly allies.

But though we had new freedoms, we also had new rules and restrictions.

Daddy's car required blue-tinted headlights, and we never turned on indoor lights without first closing the blackout curtains. All of this was so planes flying overhead wouldn't see our lights below and use us as a target.

One by one, Daddy's contemporaries slowly migrated back to the United States. Daddy had fewer meetings and we rarely entertained anymore.

Still, we managed to have fun and cause mischief, or at least partake in it. We figured out quite quickly that the building next to ours housed the Luftwaffe, with only an eight foot wall to separate our back yards. This provided hours of entertainment. Daddy liked to place our radio in the window and blast BBC broadcasts, which the Germans most certainly did not appreciate, but about which there was really nothing they could do. Jimmy's favorite broadcaster, Bruce Belfrage, seemed to mock the Germans by the very nature of his British delivery and stoicism.

One day, Annie and I found Jimmy staring through his binoculars out the window on the third floor in the direction of our next door neighbors.

"What's going on, Jimmy?" Annie asked.

Jimmy handed her the binoculars and said, "Take a look!"

Annie leaned out the window just a bit, then scanned until she gasped, put the binoculars down for a moment, looked wide-eyed at Jimmy, then put the binoculars back up to her eyes. "Well isn't *that* something!" she chortled.

At first, they wouldn't give me a turn to look, and I stood at the window sill on tippy toes trying to see over the wall and make out what they were seeing. But soon enough, I figured it out from what they said through their giggles.

"Oh let me see, already!" I said, and shoved Jimmy a little.

"What are you shoving *me* for? I don't even have the glasses!"

Finally Annie handed me the binoculars and I found what I was looking for. What Jimmy had first seen, which had prompted him getting the binoculars in the first place, was a crowd of people at the building on the other side of the Luftwaffe standing on their balcony, themselves with binoculars, staring in the direction of the Luftwaffe headquarters and balcony.

Jimmy had grabbed a pair of binoculars and saw what I now saw: three naked women sunbathing without a care in the world, and quite possibly aware of their audience. They lay stretched out on lounge chairs, periodically shifting and even turning over. Apparently, the officers and soldiers weren't all business after all.

CHAPTER NINETEEN – PREMONITION

August of 1940 started off quite wonderfully. Reunited with Daddy at last, and living in the Palais d'Assche with loads of adventures still to have, we had resumed our studies with a new tutor, the niece of Daddy's secretary. She was determined that we have many hands-on experiences. One science experiment she did with us to teach us about how seeds grow was to take a lima bean, place it between two wet paper towels, and watch it sprout, which it obliged us by doing quite quickly as it caught the sun from the windows.

While Jimmy and I were tutored together, Sis, who was about to turn 14, was tutored on her own, and seemed to have grown up over the last few months with all of our travels and adventures. Daddy said she was a young woman and this seemed to prompt her to start acting more like an adult than a child with each passing day.

One of her jobs was to keep track of our provision list. One day I peeked over her shoulder as she tallied up what we had and what we could use, and wondered about the number of beans. Ninety cans compared to only eighteen of asparagus, and two of peas. There were also two bottles of grape juice, and three bottles of olive oil, which we were always running out of.

Whenever we went to the Libby plant in Lousain, we would bring home more and more pork and beans, jam, and condensed milk, which Daddy used in his coffee. We kids still liked fresh milk to drink when it was available (except for Jimmy, who was no fan). But most often, it was KLIM powdered milk.

It came in a tin can with a small key to open it. A note reminded the consumer to keep the key to help conserve precious metal for the war effort.

Because some items were not only in high demand, but simply not available, we had to make our own products, such as "ersatz" soap. The soap was made from fat and caustic soda, and never lathered. It made a pretty poor substitute for the real thing.

Along with ration cards, just like everyone else, we had also been issued gas masks. We kept our gas masks in the larder, along with our many cans of baked beans. Sis thought having them sitting in the open, on top of Daddy's armoire, was embarrassing, and appeared desperate.

Annie took her responsibilities seriously, taking care to make sure we were well-stocked on what was available, and being careful to use only what we needed. We didn't complain about single servings, even if they were small, or the sad dab of jelly on our toast. We became creative with our limited selection using the ingredients we had in as many ways as we could think of and employing different seasonings and cooking methods. If we were out of something, we never fussed.

It all became quite routine for us. But there was one item that never lost its novelty, and over which we never grew jaded—chocolate. Chocolate was a luxury, and rations were small and infrequent. In our home, it was locked away in the cabinet down the hall from the kitchen.

Annie was the only one of us three allowed to access the key and open the cabinet. Every other night, she would walk down after dinner, with us in tow, and then, with all the weight that responsibility held, insert the key, turn the lock, and remove the precious treasure.

She would hold the sacred foil-wrapped bundle of Côte d'Or with its exotic elephant, palm tree, and pyramids on the wrapping. Then she would break off one square for each of us. Finally, she would replace the ever-shrinking bundle, lock the cabinet, and we would walk slowly back, letting the chocolate melt gently on our tongues, never once biting or chewing or even sucking on it, all so it would last as long as possible.

Daddy's secretary was well aware of our deep affection for chocolate, and managed on several occasions to bake us incredibly tall chocolate cakes which she'd send with Daddy in the evenings, much to our delight.

We awoke one morning to find Daddy in the kitchen making omelettes. We were quite surprised, having become accustomed to Hilaria Suarez y Suarez singing and cooking away in the kitchen, making the most of what food we had and teaching us skills both useful (making bread) and completely unnecessary in every way, but quite fun (how to balance buckets of water on our heads).

When we had returned from our travels, Hilaria Suarez y Suarez had returned to her duties as our cook. Every morning we'd find her there, cooking something hot and brewing coffee. So it was quite a surprise to find her gone.

"Where is Hilaria?" we all asked at once. "Is she sick?"

Daddy expertly flipped the omelette and asked us to take a seat. "I have some rather unfortunate news," he began.

My first thought was that Hilaria Suarez y Suarez had been in an accident or been arrested by the Nazis. But in either of those scenarios, Hilaria would have been the victim of circumstance and cruel fate. This turned out not to be the case.

"Listen my dears," Daddy began, as he slid plates in front of us, each with a quarter-portion of the omelette, which steamed aromatically. "I know how fond you were of Hilaria, but I'm afraid she's been stealing from us and I've had to let her go."

We sat stupefied, ignoring for the moment the savory smells coming from our omelettes, despite our grumbling stomachs. Then, we all started talking at once. I'm not sure who said what, but there were lots of, "that's not possible"s and "she would never!"s.

Then Daddy explained he'd discovered our lovely cook taking bread home to her family. He explained her reasoning. They were hungry, and had even less than we did. Daddy said it was a tough decision, but he simply could not tolerate her taking from our family's rations in order to feed her own. And therefore, he'd had to let her go.

We were quiet for a moment as the news set in. I was sad to lose our cook; she had become a member of our family. And I thought about her family, if only briefly, whom I'd never met, and felt a twinge of empathy for their hunger and need.

But it's an interesting thing, not having enough. You think you want to share and help others, but sometimes, it is your own survival that takes over, and the thought of us not having enough to eat because of her actions, even though a few missing loaves of bread really wasn't going to put us in threat of starvation, sent up our natural self-preservation flags. We didn't spend a lot of time debating the situation's moral ambiguities.

Then Jimmy asked, "But Daddy...do you even know how to cook?"

Daddy laughed, and gestured to our omelette shares, temporarily forgotten, but now suddenly the only thing we could focus on. We dug in, our enthusiasm part curiosity and part satisfaction of the salivating they had produced. It wasn't half bad. In fact, it was quite good.

After that, Daddy took to making homemade bread himself, and oh, the most wonderful Western omelettes with potatoes and ham and onions whenever those things were available. Annie took over some of the cooking too, and we all chipped in where we could, turning it into a fun family activity rather than a chore.

It was around that same time that Mr. Sussdorf out of Antwerp came to use the offices in the Embassy. He was a colleague of Daddy's. But frankly, we kids didn't like him much. He had a very brusque manner, and when he greeted the three of us, he seemed annoyed with our presence in the Embassy. But he was Daddy's superior, and so we were polite and smiling, though it's possible we may have made faces at him on occasion after he'd turned his back to walk away.

Towards the end of that month, Daddy had to take a business trip with Mr. Sussdorf. There was a meeting in Cologne, Germany with some other consuls from Amsterdam, Luxembourg, and Berlin, to name a few.

On the morning of their departure, we were eating breakfast and rather lazily lounging in our pajamas. Daddy came in to say goodbye, which had become difficult for all of us ever since our separation back in May when the Germans had first entered Belgium.

Daddy kissed us each on the head, promised to be back soon, then walked with Diany towards the door. There he said to her, "I have no faith in Mr. Sussdorf's driving. I would prefer to take my President."

Diany adamantly agreed that this was the better solution, her own feelings about Mr. Sussdorf suddenly quite apparent as her shoulders stiffened and her face took on a hard and determined look. But Daddy shook his head reluctantly. He patted her shoulder consolingly, having, in the end, deferred to Mr. Sussdorf. And so he left, with Diany looking on, worried.

Later that day, as we sat down to lunch, joking and talking and eating our food, Jimmy suddenly stopped, mid-sentence. He sat bolt upright in his chair and stared straight ahead.

"What is it, Jimmy?" asked Annie. "Are you sick?"

"I just got the strangest feeling," Jimmy said. "I felt all cold inside. And now I can't stop thinking of Daddy." His eyes darted back and forth between us, and an uncharacteristic sense of urgency had crept into his voice and posture.

"He *is* coming back, Jimmy," said Annie. "He'll never leave us again for long." But she looked quite pale and ghostly, her own forehead now creased with anxiety.

"He is only at a meeting," I said, adding my own opinion, but suddenly desperately wanting Daddy to walk through the door. Nothing felt right all of a sudden. No one finished their lunch, and our attention was unfocused and our moods slightly irritable as the day went on.

All through the afternoon, we worried about Daddy as we went about our business, reading, helping with chores, and thinking about what to make for dinner, if distractedly. Ever since food had become scarce, it was not uncommon for us to start thinking about our next meal as soon as we'd finished the one before.

But our enthusiasm for our dinner was greatly diminished that evening. We barely had energy and motivation for some cold chicken and bread. It had been a hot day, and cooking something didn't sound appealing, coupled with our growing sense of dread as we waited to hear from Daddy or see his return.

We sat down to our humble meal around 7:00 p.m. Diany hardly touched her food, claiming that she wasn't hungry because of the heat. We all sort of picked at our plates and pushed things around, but didn't do our usual devouring of every crumb. Our conversation had dwindled throughout the day as we'd grown weary of putting up fronts for one another, and our own personal worries and imaginations had taken hold.

We had just started cleaning up the supper dishes when the doorbell rang. Diany looked at all of us, then wiped her hands on her apron and started down the two flights of stairs to the first floor. We followed behind, at a cautious distance. As Diany approached the door, we three sat on the steps, arms around each other's shoulders, waiting to see who was there.

She opened the door to find Mr. Gilbert, the U.S. Vice Consul, on the doorstep. He looked rather grim, and couldn't maintain eye contact with Diany. His eyes flashed briefly to us kids, and he stood briefly transfixed, suddenly frozen to the spot.

Diany watched his face as it morphed from gray seriousness to green dread, and she slowly backed away from the door. Mr. Gilbert stepped hesitatingly in, closing the door behind him, his eyes on the floor and his lips slightly pursed.

"I am so very sorry to have to tell you this," he started, clearing his throat and sounding a little froggish.

Diany began shaking like a leaf.

"I have some bad news," he continued.

Diany's hands went up to either side of her face and she started breathing hard. I felt Annie's hand squeeze my shoulder and her body tense beside me.

"Today, right around noon, Mr. Sussdorf and Mr. Broy were in their car when they were hit by a train."

We all gasped, and Diany leaned against the wall, barely able to hold herself up.

"It was in Bergheim-Erft, near Cologne," he continued.

Diany began stammering nonsensically, and we three kids huddled together on the stairs. I began to shiver uncontrollably.

Mr. Gilbert, seeing that Diany was on the verge of collapsing, took her by the arm and escorted her back up the two flights of stairs to her room. We followed soundlessly. There, he reported that Mr. Sussdorf was dead and that Daddy had been gravely injured.

Diany kept nodding her head and saying, "Yes, of course," and staring at Mr. Gilbert as though he had three heads. Her breaths were coming in short gasps, and her face was drained of color, with a thin sheen of perspiration covering it.

Mr. Gilbert finally left, with many apologies for bringing such news and offers to return in the morning, but he also seemed to crave nothing more than a speedy exit. Diany began sobbing uncontrollably, falling against her pillows, unable to look at us, the sheets clenched in her hands.

We kids were also reeling from the news, and experiencing equal parts abject fear and a sinking feeling of having been thoroughly abandoned by any responsible adults. Diany had become quite ill from the news and could not get out of bed, so we had to get ourselves to bed that night.

I don't remember if we managed to put on our pajamas or brush our teeth. I don't remember if we hugged or reassured each other. I only recall that it felt as if I were in a dream where everything was moving both too slowly and too quickly. Sis was crying without admitting it, staying stoic as she wiped her tears away. Jimmy seemed lost and angry, kicking his bed when he bumped it accidentally. I kept asking, "But when will we see Daddy?" But no one knew and no one answered.

All through the night, we could hear Diany sobbing into her pillow. None of us slept much. In my dreams, I heard the sound of distant train whistles. They sounded either loud and shrieking, with an urgency and threat to their tone or lost and mournful, as if muffled by fog and miles. When I woke, it was with the dual sensations of an urgency bordering on hysteria and a hopelessness that felt like a dull and heavy weight upon my heart.

CHAPTER TWENTY – RECOVERY

The next week went by in a haze. Diany had been robbed of the ability to do much of anything, but she did manage to telephone the Vice Consul every day to get as much news as she could. Those phone calls were her lifeline, and she never missed them, feverishly dialing the number, with an almost visible effort to push herself into the mouthpiece itself to get closer to the voice on the other end, closer to finding out about Daddy via his nurses.

The updates she received were all pretty much the same. Daddy was in a German hospital in Bergheim-Erft. He had broken all the bones on the right side of his body and his hip and ribs had been crushed. His right eye had been severely damaged as well and there was little hope of his recovering his sight through it.

I couldn't (and wouldn't let myself) imagine the pain he was in; instead I thought ceaselessly of what it must look like to be in so many bandages. I imagined a mummy-like figure encased in a shroud of plaster and cloth, sleeping like the dead or moaning like a spook.

The German Ambassador telephoned every evening, muttering reassurances and making benign offers of doing "whatever we needed." Diany would whisper her thank yous, and we all would huddle together, wondering what anyone could do short of miraculously curing our Daddy, or at the very least bringing us all back together, which we desperately desired.

We had a never-ending train of visitors. And though they seemed to call to us from the other side of a muffled wall, it was of some small relief to not be completely alone with ourselves and our governess, who was functioning on as little effort as possible.

Mr. Pennrich (a colleague of Daddy's) and his wife were frequent visitors, doing their best to divert us with games and stories. We would politely listen and participate, even forcing smiles and feeble laughter, if only to appease them as they tried to cheer us up.

I found myself wondering as I lay wide-eyed on my pillow one night, too frightened and lonely to sleep or dream, if Mummy even knew that Daddy was injured. We hadn't heard from her in many weeks, and I didn't know who would call her and let her know. I tried to puzzle out if that was something we kids should be trying to accomplish. But I couldn't get past the wondering stage and decided not to bring it up to Jimmy or Annie, thinking if it was important, they would think of it too and take care, somehow, to make it happen.

As I drifted haltingly into a dreamless slumber, I felt no warmth or security, only a numbness that I finally gave in to, seeking refuge in the one place where I didn't have to pretend to be happy.

Meanwhile, the necessary arrangements for us to go see Daddy were slowly being put in place. Diany packed up Daddy's clothes as well as many of our belongings, not knowing how long we would be gone or even if we would be coming back. She worked with an energy that had been missing since we'd first heard the news, efficiently carrying out each task with purpose.

One afternoon, a young German soldier showed up at our door. Unlike the other Germans we'd come into contact with, this one greeted Diany with a casual familiarity that was disorienting. He smiled at her and greeted her by name, as though they'd met before. Had he been a friend from her childhood in Malmedy, we wondered? Or perhaps she'd met him on her errands around town. She stood stiffly but smiled a small smile, allowing her eyes to meet his briefly, if reluctantly.

"I will return shortly," she told us, allowing the soldier to escort her to his car. He drove her to the Embassy to fill out some paperwork we would need before we travelled to Germany. She also had to get money to pay our tutor, as well as for food and other necessities.

When she returned a couple hours later, her face was flushed. I wondered if it had been a lot of exertion to take care of all the paperwork, or if she'd been asked embarrassing questions while at the Embassy.

Finally, on Sunday, September 8th, two cars came for us. One was one for our luggage, and one for us. We were packed, prepared, and desperate to get to Daddy's side. Before we crossed the border into Germany, we stopped for lunch on the grass. Our driver, a young handsome soldier with eyes the color of the sky and lashes he seemed to think masked his fervent gazes, kept looking at Diany when he didn't think anyone was watching. But I was. She seemed completely unaware.

When we climbed back into the car after our picnic, Diany had a faraway look in her eyes, seeing nothing but whatever she was imagining in her mind. Jimmy and Annie were looking out the windows at the countryside, or maybe also imagining our imminent reunion, but I saw our driver watching Diany in the rearview mirror as he started up the car and we continued on our way.

He had been a gentleman for our entire trip thus far, but something in his eyes had a hungry look, where all propriety momentarily dropped away. Something must have alerted him to the attention being paid by this unlikely observer, for when he noticed that I was watching he quickly returned his eyes to the road. I didn't catch him peeking again during the trip.

We arrived at the Maria Hilf Krankenhaus in Bergheim-Erft at around 4:00 that afternoon. We were received by the nuns who ran the klinik, and not Daddy's doctor, Dr. Wirtz. They were all quite accommodating and conciliatory, smiling kindly, reassuring us and leading us to Daddy's room with lots of gentle warnings that he tired easily, and not to get him too excited.

After much discussion, it was decided that I should enter first. Upon reflection, I can only imagine this was because, as the youngest, it was less likely I would be overly dramatic and cause an upset. This would then somehow set the stage for the others, easing their way.

As I entered the room, I could see Daddy was covered in bandages. He couldn't move much, all bandaged up and in pain, but he watched me with his one unbandaged eye as I approached his bedside.

Trying to think of something to say, I recalled reading the side of a cereal box that had promised to help keep one fit and healthy when consumed regularly. Using what little information I had gathered about what "being healthy" meant and understanding that, at present, Daddy was not in perfect health, I finally blurted out, "Have you been regular?"

This elicited a pained groan from Daddy who tried to smile with his mouth, but only managed to with his eyes. Behind me at the door, Diany, Annie and Jim all remained quiet, but the nurse snorted and muttered a not unkind, "Oh dear."

Daddy reached his good hand out, lifting his fingers in a way I knew meant to come closer. I did, and gently wove my fingers through his.

One by one the others entered the room, coming to his bedside to take turns holding his left hand and gently kissing his left cheek. We were all a little teary-eyed. He just kept saying our names, sounding gravelly and muffled, but with an undeniable emotion that I knew was deep love. Diany stood back a bit, but his eye met hers, and something I couldn't quite interpret passed between them. She was crying and smiling at the same time, as if it hurt just a little, this joy of reunion.

Not wishing the gathering to become too morose, I decided to test out my political acumen, asking Daddy if he planned to vote for Roosevelt or Willkie in the next election. Everyone laughed at that.

Daddy then sent for the soldiers who had brought us. It wasn't a command or request so much as a questioning look in his eyes, a vague sweeping of his good arm and hand to emcompass we four, and a slurred, "How?" Once we guessed his intent and told him of our travel specifics, he managed, "See them, please."

Daddy thanked both soldiers warmly and repeatedly. He wanted to shake their hands, but the Germans remained uncomfortably stiff and would only say, in perfect English, that it was their honor and their duty. Our driver tried to catch Diany's eye before leaving, but she was focused on only one point, and that was Daddy.

Though we didn't want to, we eventually had to leave Daddy to get settled in at the Mertens Boardinghouse. We had three little rooms: one for Jimmy, one for Diany, and a third for Sis and myself. It was run by a German officer who knew of the reason for our visit and was kind in a remote sort of way, and spoke to us in respectful tones.

There was a lovely little restaurant nearby, Restaurant Rossler, with plentiful food and good service. We took all our meals there. The only problem was, we thought they were re-using the oil every time they cooked, as it tasted quite fishy, and possibly rancid. Still, because our thoughts were swarming around being with Daddy as much as possible, re-used oil was not our most pressing issue.

In the following weeks we fell into a routine that orbited around Daddy and seeing him get better. At first we'd wake up, eat our fishy breakfast, and take our walk over to the klinik. There, we'd spend our mornings with Daddy, returning to the Restaurant Rossler for a fishy lunch and some free time.

In the evenings, after our fishy supper, we would return to the klinik. We would light the way with our special flashlights with the blue screens, as there were blackout conditions in Bergheim-Erft, just as there had been in Brussels. As we became more comfortable with the small town and our routine, we took turns visiting Daddy.

If not for the somber reason for our visit, we might have enjoyed Bergheim-Erft more. The river Erft, which gave the town its name, flowed through the foothills of the Eifel, west of one tributary of the Rhine river. We would sometimes visit the river and dip in our toes, as the early days of September were still warm. Our daily walks to the klinik took us through a lovely street lined with shops and the Hotel zur Krone, which had its own restaurant.

At the far end of the town's main street stood a brick archway, the Aachener Tor. In its more than 100 years, it had been a fortification to guard the way between Cologne and Aachen; a prison (and home to a warden); and a museum. But always, it had been a strong symbol of the "gates to the city." Walking beneath its arch felt like stepping into a story.

Jimmy asked repeatedly if we could go inside and stand guard over the city, despite Diany, Annie, and our host assuring him it was neither a fortress nor a playground.

At first, the children in the town were none too kind. They threw stones at us, thinking us English. By this point, Germany and England had been warring enemies for over a year.

Once they discovered we were Americans, however, they befriended us immediately. Jimmy made friends with a group of boys he played ping pong and soccer with. Back in our rooms at the boardinghouse, Jimmy said all the German children were brainwashed Hitler Youth members.

"What are Hitler Youth?" I asked, guessing only that they were young and either admired Hitler or somehow behaved as he did.

"They haven't a thought of their own," declared Jimmy, rolling his eyes heaven-ward. "They sound like recordings with their talk of strong nations and Germany's impeccable model of how people should look and think and be." He sounded quite disgusted.

But when he was outside with the boys, Jimmy showed no hesitation or disdain. Hitler Youth or not, they were boys—boys the same age as Jimmy. Jimmy hadn't had any friends to speak of for quite some time, having spent most of his time with we three females. So despite "political differences," Jimmy took full advantage of the opportunity to bond with them, at least on an athletic and entertainment basis.

We noticed that all the boys we saw in the town were about Jimmy's age or younger. We didn't see any older boys. Diany told us that boys aged 14-18 were recruited into military camps for training as future soldiers. Jimmy was 13 by this time, and no matter how I tried,

119

I couldn't picture him as nearly old enough to carry a gun or even march in a line.

In addition to the blatant lack of older boys, Nazi flags hung at the hospital and in front of the town hall. Bergheim-Erft was a small town, and wasn't currently housing troops of German officers and soldiers, so there wasn't quite the pageantry and hanging of wall sized banners everywhere that some occupied towns and larger German cities boasted.

Daddy received many visitors during his stay in Bergheim-Erft, including Mr. Klieforth, the Consul General in Cologne, as well as the Spencers, our friends from our trip to Bordeaux. When we saw Dr. and Mrs. Spencer, we ran and hugged them.

It seemed the doctor and his wife had put aside whatever differences had arisen during our stressful train ride so long ago. Dr. Spencer offered his own medical opinion on Daddy's state of recovery, saying he was healing quite nicely. By now Daddy had no pain in his leg, and his ribs were mending well. This fortified our hope.

One of the doctors at the klinik whom we came to know, Dr. Spigelnagel, had a magnificent estate in Bergheim-Erft. Sometimes his wife invited us to tea. The house was atop a little mountain and surrounded by gardens and orchards.

They were both lovely people, gay and entertaining, and even spoke a little French. Their dog was named Strumph, and Mrs. Spigelnagel said Strumph had the same laughing eyes as Diany. We kids laughed and laughed at that. We'd never thought much about whether Diany's eyes laughed or not. But then I started watching Strumph and Diany both, and do you know, I believe Mrs. Spigelnagel was correct. There was a twinkle they shared and a glisten when both were happy.

Poor Diany. After we had been in Bergheim-Erft for a month, she received word that her father had passed away. She could not leave us (nor did she want to), and travel was difficult, so she was unable to attend the funeral. She was overcome by grief, and this was the first time we noticed any deviation from her steadfast focus on Daddy's recovery.

To pay her respects and grieve in private, she went to the small Bergheim-Erft church at the hour of her father's mass to pray alone. Some days later, she read to us from a letter she had received from her uncle. He wrote that the entire village of Malmedy had turned out for her father's mass, and there had even been a funeral procession. When pressed for details, Diany explained that the villagers processed down the main streets of Malmedy, her father's coffin on a cart, and brought it to the cemetery for burial.

Apparently, this was an honor and brought some small comfort and pride to Diany, knowing so many had accompanied her father's body to its final resting place even when she could not. Her eyes were brimming with tears, but she had a gentle smile on her face as she told us some stories about her father and took solace in the respect he was paid after death.

* * * * *

After that first month in Bergheim-Erft, we started noticing great improvements in Daddy. He was able to move a little, and was in less and less pain with each passing day. He continued to recuperate through the month of October, and on October 22nd, 1940, Daddy took his first steps.

He was taking lots of medicine to help with his pain, which made it possible for him to move at all. With those first steps, Daddy made his way, slowly, painfully, and with nurses and all of us at his elbows and behind him, to the window. I knew he must have been missing being able to look outside of these walls he'd been limited to for almost two months.

We stood with him, breathing in fresh air and pointing out different buildings. We showed him the path we took each day to the klinik from our rooms down the road.

I felt so proud of Daddy, and so excited that he was getting better every day. At times, I looked around to see whose eye I could catch to see if they were nearly as excited as me. Sometimes it was Jim Bill or Annie; other times Diany or one of the nurses. But one set of eyes I never saw were Mummy's. Since our relocation to Bergheim-Erft, we hadn't heard a word from her. I still didn't know if she had any knowledge of Daddy's accident. I wondered if letters sat waiting for us back at the Palais d'Assche, or if the mail simply wasn't reaching Germany, and somewhere in the back of my mind, if we weren't just a little guilty for not contacting her with the news.

* * * * *

By early November, Daddy was taking walks to the Mertens Boardinghouse and the Restaurant Rossler. The doctors said his eye had progressed as well. Of course, now that Daddy was better, he was wanted back in Brussels and back to work. It seemed the tabs they'd been keeping on him went beyond pure concern, and we received word that he should return to his post by mid-November.

We left on November 16th as soon as Daddy had received his passport and papers. A car came to get us, and when Daddy walked out of the klinik, limping and with the help of a cane and all of us buzzing about him like friendly but insistent flies, people hung out the windows and cheered. Doctors and patients alike were so happy that Daddy had had made such remarkable progress. He had had hip surgery during this time, and apparently it had worked.

CHAPTER TWENTY-ONE – ENDINGS

After we returned to Brussels and the Embassy, we tried to live our lives as normally as possible. Daddy was back at his post as Consul, but because of all the hurts he'd sustained in the train accident, he could handle only single tasks such as signing papers.

He tired easily, and still walked with a limp, sometimes using a cane. He came home moving slowly and needing to sit or lie down. We children would take turns rubbing his hip, which ached much of the time, and bring him hot or cold drinks, depending on his needs.

Huck kept a bottle of red wine on the bedroom fireplace mantle, and we'd pour him a glass on occasion. His other favorite request was pickled herring, which was stored in the basement. It was dark and just a little scary in the basement, so I did my best to find other things I could do for Daddy instead. If pressed, I would have Jim or Annie accompany me.

One evening Jim Bill, who was sitting in a nearby chair, read from a book and periodically showed Daddy some pictures to keep his mind off his aches and pains.

We also had the radio, still a companion, familiar and sure, like an old friend. Daddy and Jim Bill still preferred Bruce Belfrage to any other BBC correspondent. We learned after the fact that when Daddy had been recovering in the klinik, a German bomb had exploded at the BBC in London while Mr. Belfrage was doing a broadcast. It killed seven people but he was unaware of the attack since he was in a basement studio and finished his reading of the news.

While we were passing the time, we suddenly smelled something burning in the kitchen. Jimmy jumped up from his seat and licked his index finger, pointing to the ceiling. "Looks like it's coming from the kitchen. And by the strength of the stench, I'd say Annie has burned the dinner again."

With Hilaria gone, and Daddy unable to stand for long or use his right hand very well, Sis had taken up most of the cooking. It wasn't as tasty as Hilaria's or Daddy's cooking, but she did her best, and we were happy for it. But sometimes she'd forget to watch a pot that was on the stove, or get distracted and leave the bread in the oven for too long, and we'd have slightly blackened, smoky-tasting results.

Whenever we could, we kids pitched in to do more around the house and to help Daddy. One of my jobs was to help make a list of provisions that we would like to be sent from the United States. The State Department did its best to fill our requests, though it wasn't always possible. I was particularly taken with the idea of something called "peanut butter." I imagined it somewhere in the realm of caviar to be spread sparingly on crackers. I'd place it on the list, ever hopeful it would arrive from the States. I was very much looking forward to trying it out.

Another reason we kids had to step up to our responsibilities around the house during this time was that Diany had become quite ill. She would often lie in bed, moaning softly, but trying to remain stoic. She didn't want to cause any trouble and repeatedly shooed us away saying, "Help your father. It is he who needs you now."

Eventually, Diany became feverish and was clutching at her belly in agony. She had to be hospitalized at the Edith Cavell Clinic. We visited her often and tried to cheer her up. Particularly when Daddy was at work, we'd spend entire afternoons at the clinic, reading to Diany, making her pictures, and trying to keep her spirits up.

The Clinic was famous because of its namesake, Edith Cavell. She was a British nurse who had given nursing care to allied and enemy soldiers alike, and was later executed as a traitor. Hitler ordered the Nazis to blow up her statue when he invaded Paris out of what some called a bruised ego, since it was the Germans who executed her, which made the rest of the world angry at them.

The nurses at the clinic were kind, though busy, and never fussed at us. They would sometimes give us odd jobs to do. We'd take a box of bandages to another floor and deliver them to the head nurse, or sweep the hallway. We would often take our lunch or dinner there, sitting at the table by the window in Diany's large, sunny room. The sole was particularly tasty. We were even taught how to properly filet the fish.

Diany was being treated for peritonitis, an infection of the insides of your abdomen. I never understood how Diany had gotten this infection, but it caused pain and fevers. She was being treated with sulphonamides, a relatively recent medicine, but perhaps because she had waited so long to go to the clinic, the medication didn't seem to be truly working.

We three would take turns putting cool, damp cloths on her forehead, and sometimes, as tired as he was, Daddy would return to the clinic at night with us and visit with Diany.

One night, a couple of weeks after she'd been admitted, we returned with Daddy and entered the room. Diany's skin looked gray, and she didn't have the usual beads of sweat on her forehead and chest. She lay still, not even wincing in pain as she normally did.

"Children," Daddy said, his voice steady, "please go find some fresh water and washcloths for Diany. All of you, please."

Annie herded Jimmy and me out. I was last, and I turned my head to see Daddy leaning over Diany, his hand holding hers, as he whispered something into her ear.

That night, a spring evening in 1941, Diany passed away. She had been with us since our first days in Belgium back in 1936. She was only 26 years old. Returning home late from the clinic, we kids, exhausted and emotional, sat quietly in the car. Its dim blue headlights cast an eerie, surreal glow on the deserted streets. Daddy didn't speak. He only stared into the dark, slowly taking each turn until we were home, where he retreated to his room as we all headed to ours.

*   *   *   *   *

I was walking down a long, dark hallway. There were framed pictures on the walls, faces peering down at me, casting doubtful glances or accusing stares. In the distance Jimmy's voice rang out. "Watch out for the spooks!"

Ahead, a door closed with a click. Around a corner, the ankle and skirt of a woman passed just out of my view.

"Diany? Is that you?" I walked faster, though my heart beat in fear.

"Diany?"

As I turned a corner, another door clicked shut. I walked towards it. My footsteps were loud, though I was trying to be quiet as a mouse. I stood before the door. I paused, my hand only centimeters from the knob. Inside I heard a woman's voice, a murmur, barely loud enough to hear, much less discern specific words. But I could tell she was speaking French.

I leaned in closer to the door. I fought two opposing feelings: one made me desperately want to open the door and see who was there; the other made me want to run for fear of what I might see.

"Who is there?" the voice inside called. Footsteps came towards the door from inside the room.

I backed up a step. The doorknob turned. My breath came faster and faster. A thin crack of light outlined the door as it opened in slow motion. The light was strong. I could only see a silhouette of a woman at the door. She stood firmly, shoulders squared. She smelled of flowers.

"D-D-Diany?" I stuttered.

The woman stayed silent, bright light pouring from behind her, causing a corona around her shape. She said nothing. She didn't move. And yet I felt a wave of disappointment come off of her, a palpable force that struck me and filled me with despair.

I awoke with tears on my pillow and an all-encompassing sense of emptiness.

Chapter Twenty-Two – Finalité

In July, as the U.S. prepared to break off diplomatic relations with Germany, American families were ordered to return to the States. Under Annie's supervision, we slowly began packing our things, soon to be stored while we took whatever time was needed to find permanent housing, busily marking which boxes contained household items, such as books and pictures and which contained miscellaneous items such as winter clothing and linens.

With Daddy trying to work, if in a limited capacity, and Diany gone, we were left alone much of the time. Annie was taking on more and more responsibilities now that she was the "mother in charge."

Daddy began making the arrangements for our journey back to America. I say "back," but in truth, I had never been there, though Annie and Jim had. Annie was born in Washington D.C. and Jimmy in Jamaica, though they had all (Daddy, Mummy, Annie and Jim) traveled back and forth during that time. Daddy seemed very tense about our return. I was sure he was worried about the open waters, so I asked him about the mines. He only shook his head, muttering, "Don't worry. We'll be fine." I wondered if he were saying it to himself as much as to me.

On our first leg of the journey, we would make our way to Frankfurt to join other American personnel around occupied Western Europe. We went by train, and once we arrived, waited in Frankfurt for ten days without ration cards as others arrived from Berlin.

Ration cards allowed us to purchase certain foods that were scarce during the war, such as sugar, butter, and meat. Without them, it didn't matter if you had money; only those with ration cards with coupons for a particular food could buy that food. Luckily, Daddy found a vegetarian restaurant where we could eat. He especially liked the cold cherry soup.

When everyone had arrived, we all boarded another train to Lisbon. Our first trip there had been exciting, driving along the roads with Mrs. C, breaking down in the small village with all the children, eventually landing at a beautiful beachside hotel where we frolicked for weeks.

This time, it was so terribly sad. We passed through war-torn Spain where people were starving. They lined the train tracks, begging for food. When we had rolls, we tossed them out the windows to the people who would run and try to be first. There were not nearly enough rolls for all those starving people. I wondered about the children we had seen in the village, with their eyes the color of liquid chocolate and their kind, shy smiles.

Once in Lisbon, we boarded the *USS West Point* (originally the *SS America*, but renamed when requisitioned by the military). It was July 26th, 1941. Daddy told us that only the day or two before, the ship had brought back Italian and German consulate personnel who were returning from the US because their posts had also been closed.

The Germans had put out a directive that no U-boat was to stop our ship as it crossed the sea. America was still not part of the war, and maintained diplomatic relations with Germany, albeit tenuous and disintegrating. This was a relief to me, though secretly, I wondered how the Germans could stop a mine from exploding, no matter what their intentions might be.

The voyage to New York took five days. When we weren't sleeping, we were mostly up on deck where the fresh salt air helped with any seasickness. Daddy also fed us a steady diet of wafer-thin mint candies that allegedly calmed the stomach.

We all stayed in one large state room which, though clean, was cramped. At night Daddy would toss and moan, trying to get comfortable, and often finally sit up in bed, moving slowly. I knew the aching in his bones along with what seemed to be a heavy burden of worry kept sleep at bay for him. While Annie and Jimmy slept without a care, it seemed, I often kept a silent and stealthy vigil with Daddy through the lonely dark hours.

During the day, Annie, Jim and I would search for adventure where we could best find it. This was not a simple task. The boat was full to capacity with returning Americans, and most of them adults. At meals, we'd sit with Daddy and his acquaintances, answering benign questions about how old we were, how we enjoyed travel by ship, and such. We answered politely, knowing full well they were fulfilling expected niceties before moving on to politics and talk of war.

On our own, we explored the ship as best we could, though there were many areas we were prohibited from entering. Jimmy tried to rustle up enthusiasm over the prospect of sneaking into one such "Crew Only" door, but Annie, without much argument, was able to reason him out of it.

My favorite pass-time was to look out over the wide ocean. Of course, I had seen the ocean many times from the shores of Portugal and Arcachon and other beaches. However, being out in the middle of it all with no land in sight gave me a chilly feeling of being incredibly small and vulnerable.

The water had an almost black hue most days. Daddy said it was because the water was so deep. I had a morbid fascination trying to see beneath its depths on the lookout for submarines and mines, and the occasional mermaid.

There was a makeshift game room on the main deck, frequented primarily by older men playing chess and women playing bridge, but there were several games we three would pounce on when there was nothing else to do. Cribbage became a favorite of Jimmy's, who neither Annie nor I could seem to beat. He got so good at it, in fact, that he started looking for more worthy opponents.

One afternoon after lunch, Jimmy ran to the game room only to find two older gentlemen already in the throes of a game of Cribbage. Jimmy swallowed his frustration and approached the table where they played.

The first man, who I recognized as a Mr. Babbitt, though I couldn't recall his post or his affiliation with Daddy, looked up briefly from his strategizing.

"Hello young man. What can I do for you?"

"Nothing, sir. That is to say, there is nothing you can do for me. However, I believe there is something I can do for you."

Mr. Babbitt raised his eyes and turned his head, eyebrows lifting to his receding hairline.

"I see...and in what way might that be, my young friend?" he asked, a whisper of a smile playing at the left corner of his mouth.

"Well sir, I see that you are a man who appreciates this game and all its complexities..."

"You can tell that just from looking over my shoulder for 10 seconds, can you?"

Jimmy persevered. "I can tell, because the only people who play Cribbage are those who understand it well enough to stick with it, and you and your opponent'—" and at this, Jimmy paused to acknowledge Mr. Babbitt's playing partner, who had taken a cautiously amused posture as he observed this interaction. The other gentleman nodded and folded his hands across his rather ample belly as if to say, "I'll wait."

Jimmy continued. "—you and your opponent are clearly two such men."

"I see," responded Mr. Babbitt. "And what, then, is it you think you can do for me, young man?"

"Sir, if I may be so bold, I believe I can be of service by helping you with your game."

Mr. Babbitt drew his chin into his neck and his upper lip rounded over his lower. "Do you mean to coach me then, son?"

Jimmy smiled politely (which to Annie's and my fascination, looked quite genuine).

"No sir. I don't presume that you need coaching. But begging your pardon, sir—" and here he looked again at Mr. Babbitt's as-yet-unnamed playing partner then back at Mr. Babbitt, "—I should like to be your next opponent once you win."

Annie and I sucked in our breath at exactly the same moment, as if this entire act had been choreographed. Both Mr. Babbitt and Mr. Other Man belly laughed, but not at all cruelly.

"I see! How do you like that, Mr. Stamford?" Mr. Babbitt asked his now revealed companion. "It appears you will soon be on the losing end of this tête-à-tête."

Mr. Stamford, now recovering from his own braying laugh, stroked his chin quite seriously. "I propose a challenge, Mr. Babbitt. Our young friend here—what is your name, my dear boy?"

Jimmy stood a little straighter and stated quite proudly, "James Broy."

"Ah! So your Charles' son, then? Of course. I see the resemblance. Well, James Broy, my proposal is this: whichever of us wins, either Mr. Babbitt or myself—for I believe there is at least an equal chance of either happening—shall play you next. Does this satisfy your need for sharpening our skills with your own?"

Jimmy pretended to consider this proposal for a moment, pressing his lips together, and looking at each man in turn. I was duly impressed. Finally, he rocked on his feet, presented his hand to Mr. Stamford to shake, and affirmed his acceptance of the terms with a brief, "Yes, I should think that would be fine."

After shaking both men's hands, Jimmy pulled up a chair as an equal and proceeded to watch the rest of the game. Annie and I, somewhat put off by our entire invisibility during the exchange, finally left in a bit of a huff. But not without each chalking up extra points for bravery and pure genius on Jimmy's part in each of our books.

Emboldened by Jimmy's brilliant presentation, Annie and I went off in search of our own adventure. It was a rare occasion to be just us girls, and I wondered if I dare suggest something, or wait for Annie's leadership to kick in.

As we walked past a "Crew Only" door, Annie's footsteps slowed. She looked sideways at me, gave a half smile, then, leaned her back against the door and tested the latch with her hands, which she held behind her. My eyes got wide and I started to giggle.

"Shh! Bev, act naturally," Sis loudly whispered. I immediately cut short my chortling and instead pretended to inspect the fine architecture of the ship.

I heard a slight click, looked at Annie's arms, hands hidden behind her back, then up at her face, a question on my own. "Well?" I whispered loudly back.

"It's open." She stated it matter-of-factly. We then stood for what felt like an interminably long time, waiting for, I suppose, just the right moment to pull the door open and slip inside.

I looked both ways in the narrow passage we were currently in and saw no one immediately on their way towards us. I raised my eyebrows at her, hoping she could read my unspoken message of, "It's now or never."

Annie slowly pulled the door open, looking over her shoulder into the space beyond. Then she slipped inside, with me just on her heels.

What we found inside was this. Life jackets, ropes, oars, and life preservers. Also a few First Aid kits and two boxes marked "Extra Rations."

Somewhat disappointed by our discovery, Annie said, "Well, at least we dared to go in." She then tested the latches on the First Aid kits and rations supplies.

"I supposed that now we've gotten in," I began, "it would be a waste of time if we left without some sort of token."

Annie, turned to me, surprise and a hint of delight on her face. "You're right, Bev. Jimmy will never believe us if we don't have proof."

We briefly considered a life preserver, but couldn't honestly figure out a way to get it secretly back to our room, or, once there, where it could be hidden. The same went for life jackets and oars. Ropes felt too common a prize, and First Aid kits were already placed in plain view all over the ship. That left rations.

When we had first boarded the ship, Daddy assured us there were lifeboats in the unlikely event of our needing to abandon ship, and that in each lifeboat were enough rations for everyone. He didn't state specifically what those rations contained, and my experience thus far of rations had been in limited supplies of things like meat and sugar. But I couldn't imagine that was what was packed inside these individual ration tins. Nor could I envision cans of pork and beans... too heavy and how would one heat them up on the open sea?

These boxes were apparently additional supplies...that one grabbed before jumping overboard? That only the crew had access to? Or perhaps for the captain who would go down with his ship, though eating rations just before going to a watery grave hardly seemed a consolation. I wasn't sure. Nonetheless, curiosity as to their contents emboldened us to take a can and read the list of what was inside.

7 oz Pemmican

7 oz Ration C

7 oz Chocolate

7 oz Malted Milk

"Pemmican? Ration C? What could these possibly be?" queried Annie, as much to herself as to me. I think she thought herself quite the connoisseur of foods, and to come upon something she'd never encountered had her a bit flummoxed.

"Should we open it?" I asked, a little wary of her response.

Annie thought for a moment, then said, quite matter of factly, "No Bev. I think we would only be disappointed. I can't imagine the chocolate is much good, and 7 ounces of anything doesn't impress me as enough to live on."

She replaced the tin, careful to set it exactly as she'd found it. Then she rested her ear against the heavy metal door. Satisfied that no one was just outside, she inched the door open a thin sliver and peeked out.

"But aren't we taking one? To show Jim Bill?" I asked, feeling robbed already of the feeling of superiority once he'd been presented with our evidence of tomfoolery.

"Bev, I don't think we'll be able to keep it hidden...and," and here she looked down rather bashfully,"I'd hate to rob someone of a meal if they were stranded at sea."

I thought about it for just a moment, weighing the pros and cons, before agreeing with her, if somewhat reluctantly.

Annie looked out again. "Looks clear. Let's go now," she whispered and eased the door carefully but without further hesitation. I followed her out into the passage and we closed the door and latched it.

I felt a mix of exhilaration at the risk we'd taken and a bit of a letdown at the results of said risk. Still, I was satisfied we'd had an adventure, and we continued about our day, wandering passages, looking for Jimmy, eating meals, and answering the standard questions from adults.

As we made our way across the wide Atlantic Ocean, I began to wonder, would we see Mummy? Would she recognize us? Would we recognize her? It had been over three years since she'd left. Though there had been letters, sporadic at best, and a couple of phone calls, she had, in fact, become as unfamiliar to us as a distant aunt.

Somehow, we all knew not to ask Daddy about it. But I could tell even Daddy was wondering what being on the same continent would mean for each of us. Would we live in the same house? The same town, even? Would things go back to how they were, with Mummy and Daddy co-existing, coming together only to entertain people for Daddy's work or to argue? Would Mummy still be chasing her dream of politics?

Our last day on the ship was August 1st, just two weeks and four days shy of Annie's 15th birthday. As we got near to port we rose extra early and ate our breakfast in stoic, somewhat scared silence. Daddy told us to pack up the last of our things and go to one of the lower decks. We did, but were surprised that there were no other passengers assembling. We watched as the Statue of Liberty grew larger.

From our studies, we had learned that Lady Liberty had been a gift from France, and represented a gateway to America and a symbol of America's independence from Britain. It was said to welcome immigrants and represent a new life for them. I wondered how Lady Liberty felt about refugees, and if she recognized us as her citizens since we'd been so far from her shores. And me, my first time on American soil—would she welcome me as well?

As her arm and torch rose above the skyline, and the points of her crown became more clearly visible, I felt a bit of a rushing excitement. Daddy had his arms around our shoulders and a mixture of emotions played on his face. He seemed proud of his country and yet unsure of what waited for him once there. I watched his eyes turn glassy as though he might shed some tears, but his mouth remained a grim line.

"Where is everyone else?" Jimmy asked as we were shepherded to a small area on the ship that was manned by only a couple of the crew and guarded against anyone else entering.

"We'll be getting off the ship before the rest of the passengers," Daddy answered, not looking any of us in the eye.

"Are we still going to New York?" I asked, suddenly sad that I might not set foot on its shore.

"We have a special boat, Dearsie," Daddy said absently. "We'll be arriving at a different dock."

Soon enough, a smaller boat made its way out to our ship, pulling alongside us with much tossing of ropes and yelling of orders.

We were helped on board the boat and introduced to Heath Martin, who was Daddy's nephew, the son of his sister Anna Martin. Heath greeted us, calling us "cousins." Then he and Daddy embraced and clapped one another on the backs, muttering words we couldn't quite make out over the sound of the two boats' engines.

Our boat sped away from the *USS West Point*, bouncing on the water and sending spray in what felt like a baptism. I felt the ocean more strongly beneath us in this smaller craft than had been the case on the *USS West Point*. We soon docked, but there were no families and friends waiting to greet passengers. Only some dock workers.

We spent one night in New York City, but hardly saw any of it as it had been a tiring journey, and we had a train to catch in the morning. Our hotel room was incredibly clean and looked as though it had never been used. Cellophane covered everything, the drinking glasses, the towels, even the toilet seat. We laughed to see it, and wondered at the reason. Cousin Heath said it was to keep things "sanitary."

The next morning, we traveled to Washington, DC where we moved into Heath's large farm house in Dunn Loring with his wife, two children, ages 5 and 3, and their pets, a dog, and a cat. The younger cousins hid behind their mother's legs and peeked shyly at us. The dog barked and leapt about as though we'd promised a prize, and the cat stayed out of sight for the first few days, finally coming around to sniff us at night before warming up to us enough to pet her.

Some warning in the air told us that asking about Mummy was not the right thing to do at the moment. We could only assume this was what she and Daddy had agreed would happen.

We kids slept on a second-floor sleeping porch, while Huck slept indoors. The July nights in Virginia were sticky and damp, the sound of crickets and frogs unfamiliar in our ears. Our cots (for that's really what our beds were) butted against each other. We didn't mind, though. It felt strange and impermanent to be there, even as nice as Cousin Heath and his family were to us all. Annie, Jimmy and I whispered to one another at night, sometimes reaching across the few inches of space between us to touch a shoulder, pull up a sheet corner, or feel the breath of a sleeping sibling.

*   *   *   *   *

I was sleeping on my cot but aware of every sound. Even though my eyes were shut, I could picture what was happening around me. Annie's and Jimmy's cots were empty, and the sound of the crickets was incredibly loud. Their high-pitched whirring made my head throb. It got louder and louder, crescendoing with a deafeningly high note that threatened to split my head open.

Then it stopped, and the silence was even louder. There were no sounds at all. No crickets, no frogs, no creaking shutter, no fox yelping, no rustling in the bushes of some creature, maybe a raccoon or an opossum. There was no snoring coming from inside the house, or humming from the refrigerator. I wondered if my ears were plugged somehow, the way they sometimes got when traveling in the mountains.

I found the lack of sound unnerving, and tried moving my body to hear the thump of my foot on the cot, or the sheets sliding against one another. Nothing. I tried to call out to Annie or Jimmy or Daddy, but no sound came out of my mouth.

Suddenly, the desire to not just call a name, but to scream or even howl pushed against my insides with an urgency I had never experienced before. I felt an immense pressure inside my throat and against my teeth and tongue. The words, the screams, the howls

135

were insistent. A desperation to be heard filled my head, and nothing else mattered.

Tears of frustration coated my cheeks, but still no sound. A hot prickliness came over me and I itched to tell someone, anyone, how awful it felt. But there was no one to hear me, even if the sounds could escape.

I slowly entered an exhausted state of acceptance. I lay more calmly, breathed more evenly, and released the muscles in my throat and my entire body, which had tensed up during my ordeal.

Slowly, the sounds of just a few crickets came back. Then a few more, and a few more, until the night sounded the way it had before. I turned onto my side and found I could open my eyes. There was Annie, a moonlit figure on the cot beside me, breathing evenly, her dark hair spread against the white sheets and pillow case. I reached over and felt her gently heaving shoulder as she slept, then drew back my hand and touched my own face. It was wet.

CHAPTER TWENTY-THREE – HOMECOMING

The car pulled into the driveway slowly, crunching over rock and stick and coming to a stop outside the house. The engine made a ticking sound we could hear through the open window. The passenger-side door opened and she emerged, feet visible first beneath the edge of the door, then a hand on the top of the door, and next a hat followed by a face.

She shut the door, smoothed her skirt, and walked towards the house, head high, expression unreadable. She knocked firmly three times. Annie, who had been standing by the window but backed out of view once the car door opened, walked stiffly to the door.

Annie opened the door and the two of them looked at one another, eye to eye.

"May I come in?"

Annie stepped aside and held the door as Mummy walked in, smiling at Jimmy and me with the lower half of her face, lips pressed together.

"Look at all of you," she exclaimed. "All so tall and grown up. I hardly recognize you. Why, Anne, you're nearly a woman." Here eyes went directly to Annie's bust.

Annie reddened slightly, but I couldn't quite tell if she felt embarrassment or anger.

Jimmy and I stood looking at her, not sure what to expect.

"Well, let's move into the sitting room, shall we?" She walked past Annie, through the foyer, and into a room off to the left that had chairs and a sofa. She had been here before.

We all followed and sat upright. What followed was thirty minutes of awkwardness, but none of it more than a nuisance. I felt only mildly interested in the stories she told us of her mother and sisters, of her luncheons with senators, of her day-to-day activities.

She asked us each a few questions, mostly the polite kind that one would ask of strangers. For that is, after all, what we'd become. There was an indifference on our parts, and a contained civility on hers.

And though the August air was sticky, her hair remained smooth and her brow never appeared damp.

After she left that first day, an unspoken truce between we three kids emerged. We would tolerate her visits, accept any gifts, answer any questions, and never upset Daddy afterward when he asked how our visit went. By this, I knew not to tell Daddy that her hugs felt wooden, or that my heart felt cold. There was a locked door inside me and I knew that she was curious to see inside, but wasn't going to try and break in or even lose any dignity by asking if she could pass. I also knew that Jimmy and Annie had similar doors, though Jimmy's seemed to be open just a crack and Annie's keys weren't hidden very well.

In the days and weeks that followed, Mummy began visiting regularly. Jimmy usually tried to show off a bit by bragging about something he knew how to do, like catch a baseball or do a handstand. He craved her tepid attention more than Annie or I for all the effort we put into impressing her. We softened up and smiled at her more than at first, but it was never like with Daddy. Daddy made me feel warm and soft inside, while Mummy had me watching my p's and q's and needing time before her visits to turn off the relaxed way I felt when she was gone.

Mummy had never learned to drive, so was chauffeured to Dunn Loring by either Aunt Golder or her lawyer friend, Charles Patton Henry. Daddy was anxious about her visits, but he did nothing to try to stop them. Usually he'd find something to do, either at work or outside with Cousin Heath, depending on the day and time of day.

Only once did we witness Daddy and Mummy in conversation, outside by the car while Aunt Golder sat in the driver's seat pretending to remove minute crumbs or dust from her jacket. Mummy's face remained calm, while Daddy's held just barely concealed fury. We couldn't hear their words, but there was nodding from Mummy, which we took to be a concession, so different from the past when her own voice would rise and posture would stiffen.

We engaged in the visits as much as was required, and considered them as a necessary duty, much like a visit to the dentist. Mummy did seem to be trying, and we were never cross or rude to her. Her eyes sometimes seemed kind and her words softened, but the time and distance had left a narrow canyon between us. It might be stepped over, if one persisted. But for now, we each respected the divide.

* * * * *

We were playing in the yard on a sunny December Sunday afternoon when Daddy and Cousin Heath heard on the radio in Cousin Heath's workshop that Pearl Harbor had been attacked. The next day, the United States declared war on Japan. Two days later, both Italy and Germany declared war on the United States.

I wondered about the friends we had left behind in Belgium. I wondered about all the beautiful places we'd been, and people we'd met. I wondered most about the German children who had thrown stones at us, then relented when they'd found out we were American. I sometimes dreamed they'd come to find us, angry that we'd been in their country, eating their food, and pretending to be their friends.

We quickly realized that the people in the United States had mostly felt insulated and safe from the war in Europe, but once the Japanese had bombed Pearl Harbor, their security fell away. Now we were practicing for bombing raids in school, much as we had in Belgium, hiding under our desks or finding small corners to face into.

We had started school at Western High and Gordon Junior High in Georgetown, good schools that both Mummy and Daddy agreed were superior to any in Virginia, though we had to be driven in each day by a neighbor.

Jimmy felt chagrined at the idea of wearing his shorter pants, so fashionable in Belgium, while the boys here in the States sported longer ones. Sis and I tried to fit in by chopping off our braids and wearing the shorter hair styles we saw around us at school.

We stayed on at Cousin Heath's home through the autumn and into the winter months as housing was scarce, what with the government calling so many to Washington during the time leading up to and during the war. And though the house was cramped, we soon became used to our larger family and hearing only English spoken. Cousin Heath's children, still too young to attend school, became our doting admirers, and Annie became quite the little mother to them, reading to them and sharing some of the tasks required to keep them clean and safe.

Meanwhile, Daddy's own health was suffering enough that he welcomed, albeit reluctantly, some help from Mummy. In time,

Daddy's doctors informed him another surgery would be required on his hip. A friend of Daddy's from Massachusetts, Mrs. Forrest, stayed for a short time, but we kids proved to be a handful and Jimmy, though older, had not lost any of his tumultuous ways when he didn't like a caregiver.

Aunt Bernice, whom we adored, stayed for a short time as well. We had seen her frequently since our move to Virginia, sometimes going to her apartment at the All States Hotel and having the most tantalizing meals at the cafeteria nearby.

When Aunt Bernice wasn't available, we stayed with Mummy at Aunt Golder's apartment on Connecticut Avenue. The best part of those stays was the indoor skating rink within walking distance.

During Daddy's recovery, one of the nurses at the hospital told him about a house in Arlington that was available just two doors down from her own. And so, after Daddy was released, we moved out of Cousin Heath's house into our own place at last. Our belongings, carefully stored by the Swiss government, arrived from Brussels intact, all of Annie's careful packing having paid off.

Mummy continued to visit after we moved, and was a help to Daddy as he recovered at home, helping with household tasks, cooking occasionally, or bringing him something to drink. It was strange seeing him needing her in any way. It had been so long since they'd held a civil conversation. Daddy was forced to accept her help, and Mummy was given a larger opening back into our lives.

We never talked about her time away or about Diany or what we had experienced in Europe. She seemed to know some of it, and would periodically reference, albeit peripherally, some of our adventures.

"Ah, well you must have eaten sauerbraten while you were in Bergheim," she might say after cooking us some for dinner.

Daddy was not getting better, though, even with the rest and the ministrations of Mummy and an occasional visit from the nurse. His hip was chronically painful, and his ability to work became less and less with time.

After a particularly bad night in 1943, Daddy returned to the hospital. As the ambulance made its way there, Daddy passed away, his long-ago injuries finally catching up with him. I was called out of class to be told. How he had managed to stay strong through leaving Belgium and returning to the States was a mystery. I think sometimes that he finally gave in to the idea that Mummy could take over, if necessary.

The losses did seem to pile one after the other, and yet, after all this time of losing...homes, maternal influence, Diany, a country, and now Daddy, we three had become something different, something with a thicker shell, something just a little frozen. Daddy was the biggest loss of all, and yet, what were we to do? Mummy encouraged us to pray for his soul and set our sights on the future. And Daddy must've known this was how she'd react and what counsel she would lend. And somehow, knowing that he'd made peace with it, so were we able to.

Mummy had proven herself strong-willed, independent, and at least perfunctorily nurturing. She could provide the basics, and in the end, that had to be enough.

She moved into the Arlington house after Daddy died, and we four lived as a family until Annie eventually started college and working. Jimmy snuck off to join the Army against Mummy's wishes, and I found a job at the CIA where I met my future husband Don.

But in the years between Daddy passing and us leaving home, one by one, we figured out the only arrangement that could work for the four of us, with Mummy providing some semblance of guidance, and the three of us kids a unit that knew how to function no matter who was in charge. We didn't have Daddy anymore. We didn't have Diany. We had her, and that would have to do.

We never forgot our time in Belgium or the excitement and sometimes scary recollection of times spent moving further and further from the encroaching Germans. We never forgot Diany, beloved caretaker and constant presence during those tumultuous times. We never forgot Daddy, who loved us so much he couldn't bear to be parted from us, and whose absence left the biggest hole of all in our lives. And through the years, we three, Annie, Jimmy and I, stayed close and raised our children to be close to one another. We saw Bonnie frequently and traveled with her too. We made what peace we could with Mom and with our past, and we spoke French and German to one another at times, keeping alive that time of our childhood that indelibly imprinted on us what love can mean, and might not mean, as well as the sure knowledge that the bond between us was unbreakable, no matter who entered or left the picture.

Anne and Jimmy, 1929

Huck, Jimmy, Anne, Bev, and Hoop, December 1930

Charles, Anne, Cecil, Jimmy, Beverly 1931

London, August 1932

London, August 1932

Huck with Jimmy,
Bev, and Anne,
approx. 1934

Bev, Jim, and Anne, circa 1932

Anne, Jimmy, and Bev with Charles, 1932

Christmas, 1934

1936

Cecil (on left) on wedding day
(Bonnie as child), April 9, 1925

Cecil at Buckingham
Palace, 1931

Anne, Bev, Jimmy, Hoop

Cecil, Anne, Bev, and Jim, 1936

Jimmy, Anna, Annie, Bev, Charles

Anna, Bev, Annie, Bonnie

Bonnie, Bev, Annie

Bonnie, Jimmy, Bev, Annie, Anna

Charles, Anna, Annie, Jimmy, Bev

Aunt Bernice

Bonnie, Jimmy, Bev, Annie

Jimmy, Anna, Bev

JOTTINGS FROM
Verity's Notebook

FOR the first time in history a woman is being considered for appointment as an ambassador. Mrs. Cecil Broy, aged 48, is the wife of an American Consular official. She speaks Russian, French, and German, and she has been recommended to the Secretary of State (Mr. Cordell Hull) for the post of Ambassador to Russia by leaders in the United States Senate and House of Representatives.

Originally a public school teacher and social worker, Mrs. Broy spent many years abroad with her husband at various consular posts. Her three children are studying at the American school in Brussels.

\#   *   *

The Courier Mail, June 27, 1938

To my sweetest Aunt Tolles and my cousins, Dick and Gayle with love
Anne 1938
X ∧ ∧ ∧ ∧ ∧ X

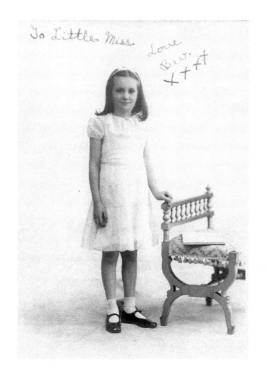

Darling Aunt Golder, cousin
Gayle and Cousin Dick,
How are you? As I
write this (the date above
is wrong) I can hear the
radio broadcasting the cheering
when Mr Chamberlain is
returning home. What do
you think of the political
situation?
Wish you were with us
Lots of love
Anne X X X

Bev, Annie, Diany,
Jimmy, Charles

Annie, Bev, Diany, Jimmy; Paris, 1939

Bride Bombed in Brussels.

We have, in these last few hours, collected some facts, many rumors and a few striking experiences. The most colorful of the latter is the hair-raising tale of a recent American bride who was on her way with her new husband to, of all places, Berlin, via Belgium, to a diplomatic post, when the latest hell broke loose. There was dog-fighting of planes at the border town as they went into Belgium—six French planes after a Nazi plane, which fled. In Brussels at the Hotel Albert Premier, on May 10, they spent a terrible night. German planes, 100 strong, came over the city in a V-shaped formation bombing all about them—the newspaper Kiosk just by their hotel was demolished. "Brussels is a rat trap," she declared. "I've been through the war!" They decided to return to France, had to get their visas for this purpose, and found the consul general who took care of them in a terrible fix with his three children, aged from 9 to 13 on his hands, his wife in America and their Belgian governess gone haywire from horror and nerves. Our bride and groom volunteered to see the children and governess safely into France. They set forth with fourteen pieces of hand baggage and two trunks for themselves and thirteen pieces of hand baggage and two trunks for the children. Their train with about 1,000 passengers reached the Bel-

THE KANSAS CITY STAR

gian frontier town safely, but just there German planes came down on the station which sheltered a British troop train. The bridegroom ordered the bride, with him and the children, to the nearest shelter. This was the first rift in marriage, for the bride refused to obey her lord and master. The fourteen pieces of hand luggage contained her trousseau and bridal linens. She declined to abandon them. So they parted with hot words— he to herd the children to safety, she to lie on her stomach in the aisle of the deserted car with her mouth open (a precautionary measure advised by her husband) for two and one-half hours while the bombs fell about.

The train eventually reached Paris. Bride and bridegroom are barely on speaking terms. But orders are for them to be in Berlin by May 15—and they are now trying their luck by way of Italy! She says it was awful —but it cost a lot of money and the government is footing the bills! (We submit this as a purely feminine reaction.)

Home these days is where you hang your gas mask . . . but Berlin is about as hard to get to as the moon.

Rumors of every disheartening description come to us.

The Kansas City Star, May 15, 1940

Diany with Jimmy, Bev and Anne at
Monte Estoril, 1940

What Comes After War

[Tom Treanor, Times staff man, now is in Europe to report the human side of the bewildering new world which war has created. His dispatches will appear from time to time under the above heading.]

BY TOM TREANOR
Times Staff Correspondent

LISBON, July 18. — The things a child notices in war are perhaps more striking than the things an adult sees. They are almost poetic in intensity. Today I talked to the three Broy children, Anne, 14; Jim, 12, and Beverly, 10; children of the American Consul at Brussels. Their mother was in Washington when the blitzkrieg began and their father, of course, could not leave his post. So they fled across Belgium, France and Spain with their nurse, a little Belgian girl who looks not much older than they are.

"I remember especially," said Jim, "that station at the French-Belgium frontier. There was an alerte and we could hear the planes with their bombs above us. People became so nervous they lit cigarettes. Then in the light of the matches we noticed that the station was almost all glass. Everybody shouted: 'Put out the cigarettes; they can see us.' I wondered what would happen if a bomb hit a glass station."

That's a picture for you.

When the first siren sounded in Brussels the children were on the eighth floor of an apartment building.

Elevator Stuck

"At first we thought it was practice," said Anne. "Then we knew it wasn't and we ran for the elevator. Somebody had gotten it stuck, so we ran downstairs, eight floors to the shelter in the basement. Nobody could find the key. An old Jewish woman kept crying. "Scandalous, scandalous."

I asked little Beverly if she cried.

"Ahem," she exclaimed in exactly the indignant tone of a French woman of 80.

"We none of us ever cried," Jim said.

They are going to Madrid to meet their father tomorrow and probably will return with him to Brussels.

"I hope it's as exciting going back as it was coming here," Anne said.

She was most afraid, Anne said, when they were stopped alongside an ammunition train. One can understand.

Suspects Locked Up

Another thing that struck Anne very funny was seeing German suspects locked up in the Brussels circus when the blitz began. In Europe circuses are permanent structures.

"The first night," Jim said, "everything was so mixed up that we couldn't tell whether the sirens were telling us the end of an air raid or the beginning. We were running upstairs and down, eight floors, all night."

They all became very merry when they remembered their first supper under bombing.

"Five times we started to eat and every time an alerte sounded," Jim said. "And guess what? Next morning we ate that supper for breakfast."

"Supper for breakfast," chimed in Beverly and rocked with amusement.

"It wasn't any too much fun missing your meals," Anne said.

In the courtyard at Palais d'Assche

Jimmy, Bev, and Anne playing in trenches behind Palais
d'Assche

Maria Hilf Krankenhaus, Bergheim-Erft; Charles' room marked
with an "x"

Annie, Jimmy, Bev, Diany, 1941

Annie, Bev, Cecil, Jim, 1948 or '49

ACKNOWLEDGEMENTS:

Thank you over and over to my memoirs writing class teacher and fabulous editor, Cecelia Hagen, as well as the other members of the class. Your contributions and questions helped move me in new directions and clarify what was not clear. Thank you David Diethelm for taking my raw digital files and turning them into A BOOK (and thank you Laura Diethelm for first introducing me to David and Eco-justice Press). Love and gratitude galore to Wendy Stasolla, my friend, cheerleader, and creative graphic designer. You brought all the elements of this story together with your beautiful cover art. And a special thank you to Pam Wilkie, who tagged along on a European research adventure, as excited as me to visit the settings of this story.

This story could not have been shared without Beverly Leidel's cooperation, remembrances, photos and clippings. Honorable mention posthumously to Anne Broy Miller and James Broy for their contributions via diary and interview, respectively, as well as Diany Jean Servais for her journal. To the generation that followed, thank you for your input and interest as this project unfolded, with special thanks to Maureen Broy Papovich, Katherine Leidel and Rachel Peck. You shared photos, read early drafts, and excitedly encouraged me. Finally, to the generation that follows my own, the grandchildren of the Broy children, thank you for the promise and hope you bring.

Photo by Jayde Silbernagel

Rebecca Norton Miller resides in Bend, Oregon with her cat Bo. This is her second publication, following a collection of poetry, *Eleven*.

Lightning Source UK Ltd.
Milton Keynes UK
UKHW031816220119
336023UK00012B/711/P